COLD CARGO

Readers are encouraged to go to www.MissionPointPress.com to contact the author or to find information on how to buy this book in bulk at a discounted rate.

Published by Mission Point Press
2554 Chandler Lake Rd.
Traverse City, MI 49686
(231) 421-9513
www.MissionPointPress.com

ISBN: 978-1-943995-59-2
LOC: TK

Printed in the United States of America.

This is a work of fiction. Names, places, and incidents are the products of the author's imagination or are used fictitiously. Any resemblance to actual events or locales or persons, living or dead, is entirely coincidental.

COLD CARGO

A MYSTERY BY
STUART SAFFT

MISSION POINT PRESS

Author's Note

The plot for this novel was developed by the participants in "Writing a Detective Novel," a 2017 summer session course I led at the Osher Lifelong Learning Institute (*OLLI*) at Furman University in Greenville, SC. The participants selected the crime, picked the victim, determined the perpetrator and motive, and outlined many of the detailed pieces of the story. In a few cases while writing the novel, I deviated from what the class came up with, but for the most part the book closely follows their outline. The names of all the *OLLI* participants are used as names of characters in the book.

I remain thankful for the participants' contributions and impressed by the cooperation, enthusiasm and creativity they displayed.

CHAPTER 1

"**D**amn. They're saying more snow again this afternoon."

"I know. It's all over the news."

"It's my parents' fault."

"Huh? How's it your parents' fault, Susie?"

"They coulda lived in Florida, rather than here in Ohio."

"Yeah. And if they did, you'd be bitching about the heat and humidity. And how inconvenient it was to always have to wear sunglasses."

"Well, maybe. But I'd like to give it a try. In any event, I'm gonna make a quick run to Kroger's. Want anything special?"

"Why doncha get a couple of frozen pizzas? And a couple of six-packs. Might as well enjoy ourselves if we're snowed in for a day or two."

"OK. Will do."

"Take my car. It's in the driveway. Haven't yet shoveled all the way to the garage. Figure I'll wait 'til Mother Nature dumps her next load, then do it all at once."

"OK."

"And take it easy driving. I'm sure some of the side roads are still icy."

"Really? Do you actually think you need to remind me? I did grow up here, you know. By the way, are you more worried about me or your car?"

"Both. Woulda clearly been you, except I just got the

car back from the body shop yesterday. That new front grille and bumper cost a fortune."

"Well, I'm honored to be up there with your car." Susie turned at the door and smiled. "OK, I'm outta here. See you in about an hour."

"Bye."

Despite expecting it, Susie Ray was still surprised at how crowded Kroger's was. *Why does everyone rush to stock up on milk and white bread whenever snow is forecast? Some secret winter recipe I don't know about?*

She was at the checkout counter 15 minutes later.

Less than five minutes later, Bobby Walthers, a tall and skinny 16-year-old boy with a heavily-pimpled face, was walking behind Ray, pushing the shopping cart to her car near the far end of the parking lot.

"Hang on, let me pop the trunk for you," said Ray as she hit the button on her key fob. She then unlocked the doors and started to place her pocketbook on the front-passenger seat.

"Oh, shit!" yelled Walthers as he jumped away from the trunk and dropped a bag of groceries, the bag splitting and vegetables bouncing and rolling every which way on the asphalt. "Ma'am! Ma'am! You gotta come here! Quick!"

"OK. OK. I'm coming. What's wrong?" asked Ray as she hurried to the rear of the car. "Oh, my God!" she shrieked as she looked in the trunk, where Walthers had been staring.

Clearly visible was a woman's body, partially wrapped in a blanket or bedspread.

"Is she dead?" asked Ray.

"I th-th-think so," responded an ashen-faced Walthers.

By then a few other shoppers had gathered around Ray's trunk. Three of them almost simultaneously called 9-1-1.

"Excuse me. Please. I'm a nurse. Let me take a look."

Enough people stepped aside so that the nurse-shopper could get right up to the trunk. She removed her right-hand glove and checked the carotid artery of the woman in the trunk. "No pulse. She's dead. Someone call 9-1-1."

"Already did," said one of the onlookers. "Cops and an ambulance are on their way."

CHAPTER 2

Meanwhile, Joe McFarland and Ginny Harris were sitting opposite each other at the small kitchen table in Joe's house.

"Sure glad it's Saturday. Hope nothing serious pops up," said Ginny. "Based on the forecast, this'll be a great day to stay inside."

"Full agreement," replied Joe. "Luckily, the heavy snow won't start until after we've had a chance to load up at the supermarket."

"We oughta do it sooner rather than later. Better chance to miss the worst of the crowd, not to mention the heavy snow."

Joe and Ginny's discussion was interrupted by both of their pagers going off.

"Looks like our services are in demand," said Ginny.

"Yeah. I'll call Dispatch and get the details while you finish dressing and putting your war paint on."

"Oh, you say the nicest things," responded Ginny as she stood up and headed for the bedroom.

Joe grabbed his cell phone and called Dispatch. His call was answered by the day-shift team leader.

"Morning, Elaine," said Joe. "You lit up our bat signals and we're ready to go. Haven't even taken the time to put our capes on."

"I'm glad that you and Robin are so responsive," chuckled Elaine Browne.

"What's up?"

"Dead body in a car trunk. Parking lot at the Kroger's, over on 8th."

"Damn. Didn't anyone read my e-mail?" asked Joe.

"What e-mail are you talking about?"

"The one where I prohibited serious crimes during inclement weather. Not to mention on weekends that we're on call."

A hearty laugh from Browne, followed by Joe asking who was first on the scene.

"Frank Marino. Arrived a few minutes ago. He secured the scene, confirmed a dead female and requested the sarge, along with the ME and the rest of the crew. Just to be sure, he also had me check that EMS was en route."

"OK," said Joe. "Ginny and I'll be on our way in a couple of minutes. Nothing like spending Saturday morning at the neighborhood supermarket."

Fifteen minutes later, Ginny pulled into the Kroger lot. The flashing patrol car lights, the tall, rectangular ambulance and the small crowd of onlookers made it easy to identify the exact location of the car with the dead body in it. Ginny pulled up fairly close to the scene, and left her flashing lights on as she totally blocked the aisle. Joe and Ginny noted that they'd beat the ME and Crime Scene folks there. But the Patrol sergeant and paramedics had already arrived.

"Morning, Sarge. Frank. Whadda we know?" asked Joe.

"Good morning, Detectives," said the sergeant. "Frank?"

"Yes, Sir. Detectives. I got the call at 10:13 and was on-scene at 10:26. Sure enough, Dispatch had it right for once. Dead woman in the trunk of this car," said Marino as he pointed to the silver Kia behind him. "I checked for a pulse just to be sure. As soon as the medics arrived, they double-checked the victim. After taping off the scene I requested the sarge, as well as the ME and Crime Scene techs."

"Whose car is it?" asked Ginny.

"A Susie Ray. She's over there, sitting in the back of my patrol car. Pretty shook up. Other than getting her basic info, I told her that detectives would be along shortly to ask her more detailed questions. I've got her cell phone here. Figured you didn't want her making any calls 'til you spoke with her."

"And Bobby Walthers is in my car," said the sergeant. "He's a young kid. One of the baggers here. Was helping her out with her groceries. He was first to see the body. Also pretty shook up."

"Do we know who the dead woman is?" asked Ginny.

"Yes," answered Marino. "Her pocketbook with her wallet and driver's license was in the trunk next to her. Name's Kathryn Knox. Lives at 143 Circle Lane here in Jasper Creek and, based on the business cards in her wallet, she is, or I should say was, the chief financial officer at National Pipe."

"OK. Well done, Frank," said Joe. "After we take a look at the vic, we're going to talk with the car owner and the bagger kid. We'll use your cars for the interviews if that's OK with you guys. And, needless to say, keep the gawkers and the soon-to-arrive newspaper and TV folks at bay. I'm sure the ME and the Crime Scene crew'll be here shortly."

"Will do."

"Joe, you called it again," said Ginny. Looking almost straight up, she pointed to the news helicopter circling some 400 feet above them. "Smile. You're on Candid Camera. Or at least on Channel 4's news bulletin."

"Hell, they didn't even give me time to get my TV makeup on," complained Joe with a half-smile.

Joe and Ginny walked to the open trunk and peered inside. Sure enough, inside was a dead, attractive female, probably in her mid-to-late 30s, dressed in casual business attire. She was partially wrapped in what appeared to be a blanket or bedspread. Her pocketbook was open and her wallet was lying next to it, the result of Officer Marino checking for the victim's identity.

Ginny put on a pair of disposable gloves and lifted the wallet. "Clearly not a robbery. Cash and credit cards still here. Also, her cell phone's still in her pocketbook."

"Hey, you must be a detective," teased Joe.

Joe and Ginny then walked over to Marino's patrol car. Joe got into the front passenger seat and twisted around to face Ray. Ginny got into the back seat and introduced herself and Joe. Joe's first thought was how nice and warm it felt to be sitting in the car, with its motor running and the heater blasting on high.

"We'd like to ask you a few questions, Ms. Ray," said Ginny.

"Sure. Go ahead. But I got more questions than answers, so I'm not sure how much help I can be."

"Why don't we start by you walking us through what happened this morning?"

"OK. We got up around 7:30, showered and dressed and had breakfast. We always watch the news over breakfast. And we saw that more damn snow is forecast for this afternoon."

"When you say 'we,'" asked Joe, "who was with you?"

"My boyfriend, Rick. Rick LaCroix."

"You two were together all morning?"

"Uh, yeah. We've been living together at his house. But it's not what you think. We're planning on getting married soon."

"OK. Please continue," said Ginny.

"So I decided to make a run to the supermarket before the snow returned."

"And?" prompted Ginny.

"That's what I did. I was returning to my car, and the bagger was helping me with my bags. I popped the trunk. He lifted the lid and screamed. I rushed over. And I saw the body. I think I screamed also."

"How did the body get into your trunk?" asked Joe.

"What? I have no idea."

"When did you last open the trunk before this morning?"

"No idea."

"Was it recently? The last few days? Or weeks ago?"

"Like I said, I have no idea. It's not even my car."

"Oh," said Joe. "Whose is it? And how come you were driving it?"

"It's my boyfriend's. He left it outside the garage yesterday 'cause the driveway was only partially shoveled. So I took his car."

"Do you know when your boyfriend last opened the trunk of his car?" asked Ginny.

"No idea."

"Ms. Ray, did you recognize the woman when you saw her in the trunk?"

"Sure. We work at the same company."

"Oh?" said Ginny.

"Yeah. She's Kathryn Knox, the head of all the finance stuff at National Pipe. I'm a lead operator in the plant there. We weren't friends or anything, but we knew each other."

"Any other ties to her? Can you think of any reason why her body would wind up in your boyfriend's car?" asked Joe.

"No, I can't. Maybe you should be asking him. He might know."

"Why do you think he might know?" asked Ginny.

"Well, they were married for a long time."

"Oh. When was that?"

"They got married almost 20 years ago, then got divorced a couple of years back."

"Because of you?" asked Joe.

"No. Definitely not! I mean, I knew Rick from work, but we didn't start dating 'til after their divorce."

"Your boyfriend also worked at the same company?" asked Ginny.

"Yeah. He was in charge of quality control. But he quit soon after their divorce."

"Ms. Ray," said Ginny, "we're going to want to speak with your boyfriend. We can drive you home and question him there. We'll need to keep his car for a few days. Just give us a few minutes to talk with the bagger who was helping you, then we'll be ready."

"OK. Can I call him and tell him what's going on? He'll be getting worried by now."

"Sorry. no. We'd rather you not call him. You can explain everything to him when we get there. It won't be long."

"OK."

Ginny walked over to Officer Marino and asked him to sit with Ray until she and Joe were finished talking with Walthers. She told Marino that he could return Ray's phone to her, but to make sure she didn't make or answer any phone calls.

Joe and Ginny spent the next few minutes in the sergeant's patrol car, speaking with Walthers. He was still in a state of shock. He confirmed everything that Ray had said about finding the body, but didn't add any new information.

Joe and Ginny then spent a few minutes with the sergeant, talking with him about maintaining the integrity of the scene and arranging for the car to go to Forensics. "When he arrives, tell the ME that we'll be in touch, probably after lunch," Joe said.

A few minutes later Ginny drove off, with Joe in the front passenger seat and Ray sitting behind Ginny.

CHAPTER 3

Fifteen minutes later, Ginny pulled up to the curb in front of LaCroix's house. It was a small Cape Cod, with white siding and emerald green window shutters and front door. The small lawn was covered with snow, but six or so evergreen bushes could be seen along the front of the house. Ray, Joe and Ginny all got out of the car and started up the shoveled walk to the front door. Before they were halfway there, the front door opened.

"My God. Susie. Are you OK? What took so long? Who are these people? Where's my car?"

Ray ran forward, hugged LaCroix and began crying on his shoulder. Joe and Ginny reached the front door and stood there silently for a few seconds.

"Excuse me, Mr. LaCroix. I'm Detective Harris, and this is Detective McFarland. We've got a few questions for you. May we come in?"

"Uh, yes. Sure. Come in." LaCroix let go of Ray and led everyone into the living room right inside the front door. "Sit down. Please. What happened? What's going on?"

Joe and Ginny sat in two end chairs, while LaCroix and Ray sat next to each other on the couch.

Joe briefly summarized the morning's events to LaCroix, with several interruptions and added comments by Ray.

LaCroix looked surprised at the news, but Joe and Ginny couldn't be sure if it was sincerity or good acting.

"Was it really Kathryn Knox?" asked LaCroix.

"Yes, I'm afraid it was," answered Ginny. "We understand that you two had been married. Is that correct?"

"Yes, for about 15 years. Then she dumped me two years ago. Out of the blue. For no reason. She just walked out."

"We understand that you also used to work with her at National Pipe?"

"Yes, that's right. When they were recruiting her to move here to be their CFO, they offered the QA manager job to me as an inducement for her to accept the job. I have a lot of QA experience, so it wasn't just a recruiting ploy."

"And we understand you resigned soon after your divorce."

"Yeah. I was really steamed. And seeing her every day at work was getting increasingly unpleasant."

"Was it an amicable divorce?"

"Hell, no. The only good part is that we didn't have any kids. She fought over every item, making a big deal of almost every damn plate. And she vigorously fought paying me any alimony. Even though she was pulling in about four times what I was making. Not to mention all the sacrifices I made early on, supporting her through college and her MBA, and sacrificing my career as we moved around so her career could advance."

"How'd she wind up in the trunk of your car?" asked Joe.

"I haven't got the slightest idea."

"When was the last time you'd opened your trunk?"

"It was just a week ago, in fact. Last Saturday morning I

went to Home Depot to buy more bags of salt. For ice on the driveway. She surely wasn't in the trunk then."

"Who had access to your trunk over the past week?" asked Joe.

"Well. Clearly Susie and me. Plus, the body shop guys."

"Body shop guys?" asked Joe.

"Yeah. I skidded into a tree a couple of weeks ago. Damn ice on the road. Luckily, I was going slow. Once I worked through all the insurance BS, I took it into the body shop. They kept the car for two days to fix the front end. I got the car back yesterday afternoon."

"And who at the body shop had access?"

"You'd have to ask them. I'd guess most or all of their employees. They all had access to the keys, I would think. Or they could pop the trunk open from the switch under the dash if the car wasn't locked."

"Which body shop?" asked Ginny.

"Sunshine Auto. Hold on a sec. I'll get you their card."

LaCroix left the room and was back a minute later. He handed a business card to Ginny.

"Thanks."

"Anyone else with access to the trunk?" asked Joe.

"Just about everyone. When the car's in our driveway or garage, we almost never lock it. One of the few perks of living in a small town."

"May we see your garage and driveway?" asked Ginny.

"Sure. Follow me."

LaCroix put a jacket on and led Joe and Ginny through the house and out the back through the kitchen door. A short walk across their small, snow-covered back lawn and they were at the rear door to the two-car garage. They entered the garage. Joe and Ginny took a quick look, but didn't notice anything unusual. A car which they assumed was Ray's was closest to the rear door, and the empty space next to it presumably was where LaCroix's car was normally parked. Joe opened one of the overhead garage doors and saw the half-shoveled driveway. The entire driveway was about 50 feet long, and led to one of those back alleys which provided access to everyone's garages, but not to their houses. Joe looked for footprints or drag marks, but the recent snow had obliterated whatever may have been there.

Back in the living room, Ginny asked, "Any idea who might want Ms. Knox dead?"

"None. But I bet if you ask a bunch of people that same question, many will say me."

"Oh?"

"Yeah. Our not-so-friendly divorce was far from a secret."

"Understood. Well, I think we're done for now, Mr. LaCroix. Thanks for your time. I'm sure we'll have more questions once our investigation gets further along. Assuming you have no objection, our techs will also be by later today to carefully check out your garage and driveway. Please stay out of the garage and off the driveway until they finish."

"Fine with me. And you know where to find me. When can I get my car back?"

"Not sure," said Ginny. "I imagine it'll be three or four days until the forensic guys are through with it. You'll hear from them or us as soon as it's available."

"OK."

Joe and Ginny were back in Ginny's car. After being patched through, the sergeant at Kroger confirmed that the ME and Crime Scene technicians were still on scene. Ginny headed back there, arriving less than fifteen minutes later.

"Hi, Doc. How're ya doing?" said Ginny.

"Hi Ginny. Joe. Heard you guys were here earlier and would be circling back."

"Yeah," said Joe. "We didn't finish all our shopping yet. Any first impressions?"

"A few. Almost certainly her broken neck was the COD. Based on bruising of much of the body, along with a number of scrapes and cuts, it most likely was from a fall. Hard to tell if accidental or pushed until we have her up on the table."

"Given that she wound up in a car trunk, kinda hard to think accidental," said Joe.

"Probably right," said Ginny. "Unless it really was an accident, and somebody with her just panicked."

"Yeah. That's possible," said Joe.

"Any defensive wounds? Anything under her nails indicate she fought back?" asked Ginny.

"Nothing obvious showing. But give us time to do our thing."

"For sure, Doc. We're just trying to get a jump on things. Speaking of which, can you estimate TOD?"

"Not very well. The cold weather slows everything down. In fact, the body was half-frozen through when we got here. I'd estimate she died at least eight hours ago, and probably not more than 36 hours ago."

"Wow. That's quite a range," said Joe.

"I know. Sorry. Hopefully we'll be able to narrow the window."

"Understood. And, I was just saying. Not complaining."

"OK, thanks Doc," said Ginny. "We're gonna go talk to the Crime Scene guys. See ya."

"So long for now."

Joe and Ginny approached the two Crime Scene technicians standing by the open back doors of their van. Hellos were said all around.

"Whadda we know?" asked Joe.

"Damn little, unfortunately. The victim clearly didn't die in the trunk. She was placed in it. With no drag marks in the snow near the trunk of the car, it was most likely driven here with the body already in the trunk. We obviously have no idea where she died. Nor whether the person who drove the car here was involved, or had any knowledge of the victim in the trunk."

"Threads from the bedspread caught on the trunk frame indicate that the victim, wrapped in the bedspread, was half-lifted, half-rolled into the trunk," added the second tech.

"That's useful to know," said Joe. "Probably just one person manhandling her into the trunk."

"Or two small, weaker women," said Ginny.

"Could be," Joe responded. "Any fingerprints?"

"Quite a few. We've got 'em all, but Forensics'll need to try and identify them once we're back at the lab."

"Great. Anything else?" asked Ginny.

"Nope. That's it for now. We'll get the car to Forensics and see what else they can find."

"OK, thanks," said Joe. "Oh, and make sure they also check her cell phone, which is still in her pocketbook."

"You really didn't have to tell us that. This ain't our first rodeo, as the saying goes."

"Sorry about that. No disrespect intended. I just wanted to be sure."

"Apology accepted. No worries."

Joe and Ginny arranged for the Crime Scene technicians to meet them at Knox's house in about one hour, and for a Patrol officer to be stationed at the house to be sure no one entered it until the detectives arrived. They wanted to get an early jump on searching her house, but they were starving and decided to grab a quick lunch first. Joe also arranged for one or two technicians to check LaCroix's garage and driveway sometime later in the day. They said their good-byes to everyone working the crime, after which they walked toward Ginny's car. As they got close to the taped-off boundary, several reporters and TV cameramen scurried over to them.

"Detectives. Detectives. What can you tell us?"

"Damn little so far," said Joe, with his reporters-specific growl and scowl.

"Come on. Give us something."

Ginny jumped in before Joe could make a nasty comment. Ginny couldn't understand why Joe never gave any slack to the reporters and TV folks. *Heck, they're working folks like us, just trying to do their jobs.* "Hold on, folks. We're only just getting started. We can tell you that a dead woman was found in the trunk of that silver

Kia Optima over there. As our investigation proceeds, I'm sure you'll be getting updates from our press office. If you'll please excuse us now."

With that, like the seas parting for Moses, the reporters and cameramen stepped aside and opened a pathway. Joe and Ginny walked through the path, got into Ginny's car and headed out of the parking lot. On the way out, Joe restated how hungry he was. Ginny obliged by stopping at a KFC a few minutes later.

"Good idea, Partner. It's been quite a while since we ate at the Colonel's."

"Yeah," said Ginny. "I figured we could use a change once in a while. If we keep going to Sancho's every day, we'll turn into tacos."

"Or burritos, if we play our cards right."

After a quick look at all the menu options, they both went with Big Box Meals — chicken, mashed potatoes with gravy, coleslaw, a biscuit and a Diet Coke. Joe and Ginny took their meals to a corner table and sat down. Enjoying their lunch, they couldn't help discussing the case between bites.

"The good news, Joe, is that dying from a broken neck is virtually instantaneous. At least the victim didn't suffer."

"True. But there is a loss of dignity, even for a dead body, to be dumped in a trunk."

"I agree. By the way, it sure was considerate of the perp to provide the vic's pocketbook and wallet. Can't have it easier than that."

"Yeah. Although identifying her probably would've been pretty easy even without that. As a big exec at one of the largest companies around here, many people besides Ray would have recognized her right away."

"Yup. My guess is Ray had nothing to do with this. Don't have to be too bright to know not to open the trunk in front of that bagger."

"Right. But her boyfriend might be a different story."

"I agree with you on that, Joe. Of course, there's also anyone at that body shop, or anyone who has a gripe against the vic or her ex-husband."

"And almost anyone else, since the car was left unlocked in the driveway. Ginny, why do we always get the cases where the whole world are possible suspects?"

"Just lucky, I guess. We'll know a lot more once we do some digging into the vic's background. Also the ex-husband, and whoever works at that body shop."

"Sure hope so."

"Joe, I gotta ask you something."

"OK. Go for it."

"I think I know you pretty well by now."

"I would hope so. But what's your question?"

"How come you're always so hostile to all the reporters and cameramen?"

"I am?"

"Most definitely. And I don't get it. It's not like just one or two of them bother you. It's automatically all of them."

"Hmmm. I never quite realized that."

"You're usually very understanding of working stiffs like us trying to do their job. Except for reporters. Why?"

"It's probably an unconscious reaction to how they acted when Lori and Adam were killed."

"Oh?"

"They were like a bunch of vultures. They wouldn't leave me alone for a minute. And talk about insensitive. 'Detective, how does it feel to have your wife and six-year-old son killed?' 'What would you like to say to the drunk driver who did it?' 'What would you say to your wife now if you could talk with her once more?' 'To your son?'"

"Jeez. That's horrible. I had no idea. You never mentioned this part before."

"Yeah. Well, I guess I sort of buried it deep inside someplace. But I really didn't think it showed so frequently."

"It does. Whenever we face or have to push past reporters and cameramen. But I gotta say, you've got a damn good reason. I'm so sorry you had to put up with that, on top of all that you were going through after they were killed."

"Thanks, Partner. And I'll try to be a little nicer to reporters in the future. But no promises."

"Fair enough."

Jeez, what he must have gone through. It's amazing he eventually came out the other end in as good a shape as he did. Then, Ginny thought how lucky she'd been that she and Joe met and fell in love with each other. She chuckled to herself as she pictured what people saw when they were together: broad-shouldered, six-foot-four, rugged Joe and thin, wiry, five-foot-five Ginny. They made quite a pair.

Joe and Ginny finished their lunch, dumped the trash on their way out of the restaurant and, in light of the cold temperature and heavy snow falling, ran back to Ginny's car as quickly as possible.

CHAPTER 4

Twenty minutes later, Ginny pulled up in front of 143 Circle Lane. Knox's home was a fairly large ranch house with light brown shingles and dark brown trim. The driveway ran up the right side of the house to what appeared to be an attached two-car garage. The front lawn was small, and encircled by a white picket fence. For no apparent reason, Joe wondered whether Knox mowed the lawn herself or hired someone.

"A pretty big house for a single woman," said Joe.

"Probably her and LaCroix's house when they were married, and she snared it in the divorce."

"Bet you're right."

The two Crime Scene technicians were sitting in their van parked in the driveway, and Officer Simmons was standing by the front door. As Joe and Ginny walked partway up the driveway to the walk leading to the front door, the two technicians got out of their van, grabbed their toolkits and followed the detectives.

"Hello, John," said Ginny to the Patrol officer. "You must be freezing out here."

"Hi, Detectives. It's not that bad. I've been moving around stringing up the crime-scene tape and checking all around the house until a few minutes ago."

"That's good. We're going to wander through the place and see what we can find."

"Go for it."

"Let's all head inside. You can stand by the inside of the door a lot more comfortably than the outside. We four," said Joe, as he swung his arm to indicate Ginny and the two technicians, "will take a look around."

"Works for me, Sir."

Joe and Ginny spent a little over an hour going through the house. They looked everywhere, while focusing on Knox's home office, the kitchen, and her bedroom and bathroom. They found nothing of interest. Ginny was amazed at how neat and orderly everything in the house was. From Knox's makeup in the bathroom cabinet to her clothing in her closet to the papers in her home office, everything was perfectly in its place.

"Wow. That was one organized lady," said Ginny. "She was way past what you'd call organized. She had to have been anal, with a capital A."

"No question. I wonder if she ironed and folded her dirty clothes before she put them in the hamper."

"Yeah, and maybe also washed them first," said Ginny with a smile.

"Even the garage is meticulous. Not a single dead leaf on the floor. And everything put away neatly on the shelves or hanging from a hook. Hell, I bet her garage is cleaner than my kitchen."

"True. But then again, sometimes your kitchen . . . ."

"Gimme a break. There's only one thing wrong with her garage."

"What's that? I didn't see anything."

"Exactly," said Joe.

"Come again?"

"No car. We need to find out where her car is. That

could very well be where the crime scene is, or at least where she met her murderer."

"Good point. I'll contact her employer to get the details on her car. I'm sure someone in her position had a company car."

"Bet you're right."

Ginny called National Pipe and spoke with their after-hours answering service. She got the cell phone number of Knox's boss, a Philip Van Hale. Ginny called and spoke with Van Hale. He confirmed that Knox, along with himself and a few other key executives, did indeed have company cars. "And, yes, I know exactly what kind of car Kathryn had. To avoid any conflicts, our policy is that all of us, including me, have the very same car except for color, which the person can select for him or herself. We all have four-door Buick Regals. Wanted to be sure that our company cars were all American made, not imported. We vigorously fight against unfair imports of pipe by our competitors, and we have to put our money where our mouth is."

"Do you know the color of Ms. Knox's car? And the license number?"

"Her car is a metallic blue. I went with black for mine. And I pretty much know her license plate."

"Pretty much?"

"All of us have special plate numbers. I think that helps remind the executives of this expensive perk they're getting. All the plates are 'NP' followed by three numbers. I didn't want to cause a competition by using one, two, three and so on. So, for example, my plate is NP 618. I don't know Kathryn's exact plate number offhand, but if you need it right away I can go into the office and look it up."

"Thank you, Mr. Van Hale," said Ginny, "but that can wait until Monday. We can do everything we need to for now, knowing that it's a metallic blue Buick Regal with an 'NP plus three digits' plate."

"OK, then. Glad I was able to help."

"Thanks again. By the way, we'll want to talk with you and others at National Pipe early next week. We'll call first and schedule our visit."

"That'll be fine. We all want to do everything we can to help find the monster who did this."

Ginny and Van Hale completed their call, after which Joe and Ginny were ready to leave. The two technicians were still busy checking everyplace and collecting several bits of what looked like nothing, along with a large number of fingerprints. They also assured Joe and Ginny that they would take Knox's laptop back to the lab with them.

Joe and Ginny said their good-byes to the two technicians and Officer Simmons, and headed back to Ginny's car.

Before Ginny started driving, she called the desk sergeant and arranged for him to issue a statewide BOLO for Knox's car.

"Ginny, we really oughta interview the neighbors while we're here. But with it already starting to snow hard, I say we take a raincheck on that. Or is it a snowcheck?"

"Call it whatever you want, but I agree to do it some other time."

"Good. Now let's stop and load up at a supermarket.

The snow's only gonna get worse. Let's do our shopping and head on home. In fact, we shoulda shopped when we were at that Kroger's."

"Yeah, sure, Joe. Your friendly reporters would have loved that. I can just imagine the lead sentence: 'Detectives investigating a murder in supermarket parking lot take time out to do their weekly shopping.'"

"I know. I know. Just kidding. But it would have been convenient."

"Anyhow, we're not far from a Meijer's. I'll swing over there."

"Boy, you sure know your supermarkets."

"Just one of my many areas of expertise."

"Good to know."

They entered the Meijer supermarket ten minutes later. Joe and Ginny walked the supermarket aisles and quickly filled their shopping cart. After what seemed like an inordinate delay at the checkout counter due to all the snowstorm shoppers, Joe and Ginny were back in Ginny's car and heading to Joe's house.

Other than shoveling the driveway and front walk Sunday afternoon and paying some bills, Joe and Ginny spent Saturday evening and most of Sunday just "hanging out" in Joe's house.

Using Joe's home computer, Ginny was able to locate Knox's parents. Shaun and Nancy Knox still lived in Marlboro, Massachusetts, where Knox was born and grew up. Ginny called the Marlboro police department and spoke with a Captain Hennessey. After a summary by Ginny, Hennessey said he'd send two officers to the Knox home and inform them of their daughter's death.

Ginny gave Hennessey her contact information so that Mr. and Mrs. Knox could contact her directly.

For the rest of the weekend, Joe and Ginny were delighted to have walls and windows between themselves and the snowy weather outside.

As was often the case, Ginny couldn't help but marvel to herself how she and Joe had fallen in love. Totally different backgrounds, he growing up and initially on the job in Chicago, she having spent her whole life in Jasper Creek. Fate had surely played a role when Joe decided to leave Chicago and wound up in Jasper Creek, eventually joining the local police department.

CHAPTER 5

By 7:45 Monday morning, Joe and Ginny were sitting at their opposing desks at the police station, each with a cup of reasonably fresh coffee.

"OK, Joe, let's start digging into the backgrounds of some of our new so-called friends. But first we ought to bring the chief up to date."

"You sure know how to ruin a guy's day. But, just to show you that chivalry isn't fully dead yet, I'll go talk to the chief while you start learning more about our potential suspects."

"Why, thank you, Sir Walter Raleigh. Can I expect you to lay your coat on the ground for me in the future if I have to cross a puddle?"

"In your wildest dreams. Don't push it," said Joe, flashing a wide smile.

Ginny got to work on her computer as Joe walked back to the chief's office.

"Morning, Chief. Got a few minutes?"

"Sure. Especially if it's for something useful. Or at least interesting."

"Maybe both. Want to fill you in on the homicide we caught on Saturday."

"Go for it."

Joe summarized everything about the murder: how the body was first discovered, the identity of the victim, whom Joe and Ginny had spoken with and their next steps.

"Sounds like you're off to a good start. Let's hope for a quickie on this one."

"Chief, you know we always hope for a quickie. But our hopes don't always come true."

"Maybe you gotta hope harder. Or work harder. Or maybe work smarter."

"Gee, thanks for the great advice, Chief. We never would have thought to work hard. Or smart," said Joe with a grin.

"Speaking of smart, Joe, no need to be such a smart ass," said the chief, with what might have been a slight smile. "Why don't you head back to your partner and help her with the load?"

"On my way, Chief. We just figured you'd want an update."

"I did. And thanks."

With that, the chief returned to examining the piles of papers on his desk, making it more than obvious the time for Joe's exit had arrived.

When Joe got back to his desk, Ginny asked how his session with the chief had gone.

"No worse than expected. I'll feel better once I remove his boot from my rear end."

"Understood. Meanwhile, I've made some progress. Got a pretty good feel for the vic."

"Let's hear it."

"OK. Here goes," said Ginny. "Thirty-eight years old. Born in Marlboro, Massachusetts, about an hour west of Boston. Lived there through high school, then went to the University of Connecticut, where she majored in mechanical engineering. She met LaCroix, her future husband, at the university, where he was also a student. He graduated one year before her, and he got a job at a small tool-manufacturing company in Connecticut. They lived together in a rented apartment while she finished her last year. They married a month after she graduated.

"LaCroix then supported both of them while Knox got her MBA at the University of Hartford. They spent the next dozen or so years moving around as Knox advanced in her career. Lived for a few years each in North Carolina, Maryland and Atlanta. Each time they moved, LaCroix quit his job and found something else in their new location."

"Sounds like her career definitely took priority over his," said Joe.

"Sure does. She had the better education and, I guess, was brighter than him. Anyhow, about four years ago she was hired as chief financial officer by National Pipe."

"So her husband needs to change jobs again."

"Yeah, but it was a bit easier this time. Like he told us, as part of their recruiting effort for her, National Pipe agreed to hire him to head their quality control function."

"Nothing like riding along on the coattails of your wife. Made his job search easy, but I bet it didn't do much for his sense of masculinity."

"Probably right. In fact, from the time they first moved to Jasper Creek, Knox made four 9-1-1 calls for fighting and spousal abuse. Each time, Patrol got them separated and calmed down. And each time, Knox decided not to press charges, so nothing ever happened."

"Does her husband have a record? Doubt if he had anger issues only with his wife."

"Haven't gotten that far yet. Let me finish. I'm almost done."

"Sorry. Go on."

"She finally divorced him two years ago. Claimed incompatibility. It looks like the fighting continued up 'til the end, and was the real cause of the split. No children. But, like LaCroix told us, the divorce was anything but amicable. Remember, he said they fought over every dish?"

"Yes, I do. Anything else?"

"Here are a few photos of her that I printed from the internet," said Ginny as she handed them to Joe.

"Very attractive," said Joe. "Clearly more so than after she was killed."

"Can't disagree with that."

"Anything else?"

"Nope. In fact, I was just about to start looking into the ex-husband. Why don't you start with the body shop crew?"

"Will do. I'll head over there now, while you're wearing out your keyboard. I should be back in time for lunch."

"Sounds like a plan, Joe. See you later."

Joe got into his car and drove to Sunshine Auto. Pulling up in front, Joe remarked to himself how almost all body shops look identical: located in a rather dilapidated part of town, usually in an old brick or sheet metal building, with cars and car parts strewn all over the fenced-in lot. Joe walked through the gate opening and entered the building.

Approaching the man closest to the entrance, who was working on the rear bumper of a bright red Mazda convertible, Joe asked, "Where's the boss?"

Without saying a word, the worker pointed to the far left corner of the shop. As Joe walked toward it, he saw a large window with a cramped office area behind it. Joe walked through the door and up to the man sitting behind the desk.

"Hi. You the manager?"

"Sure am. What can I do you for?"

Joe took out his badge and ID and waved them in front of the manager. "Detective Joe McFarland, JCPD."

"Mike Delmond. How can I help you?"

Joe sat down in the one chair in front of the small desk. "Got a couple of questions for you."

"Go for it."

"Do you recall recently repairing the front end of a silver Kia Optima? For a Rick LaCroix?"

"Yeah. Last week. I think he picked it up either Thursday or Friday. Why? Is there a problem with our work?"

"Not that I'm aware of."

"Then what?"

"Saturday morning, a dead woman was found in the trunk of that car."

"What? Jeez! Don't hear that every day. How'd it happen?"

"That's what we're trying to figure out. Who here had access to that car?"

"What! You thinking someone here did it?"

"Don't know yet. We're checking everyone who could have accessed that car trunk."

"Can't believe it's anyone here. But any of us could have had access. While a car's in the building, the car's unlocked and the keys are either in the car or hanging there," said Delmond, pointing to a peg board positioned inside the office next to the door. There were about ten key rings, each with a tag attached to it, on the peg board. "When the car's outside in the lot, either before or after we've worked on it, we lock the car and hang the keys here."

"And who can get their hands on the keys hanging here?"

"Anyone who works here can come and get the keys. Sometimes I'm here in the office when they do, but often I'm not. I could be in the shop. Or outside on the lot. Or maybe not even here."

"How many employees do you have here? I'd like to spend a few minutes talking to each of them."

"Yeah. Sure. Now?"

"Yes. And I might as well start with you. After we're done, I'd like to use your office if I could, and have you send them in one at a time."

"OK."

"Mr. Delmond, is there anyone you might suspect? Anyone who's been acting strange or different recently? Anyone take an unusual interest in that specific car?"

"No to all those questions. We got a good group of guys here. Hell, we're like family."

"Can I get copies of your security camera recordings?"

"'Fraid not."

Joe leaned forward and raised his voice. "Mr. Delmond,

this is a murder investigation. We can easily get a warrant if we have to. Why not just cooperate?"

"It's not that. Our cameras haven't worked for years. We keep them hanging there, along with the 'camera surveillance' signs. I think that prevents a lot of things from happening, even though none of the cameras work."

"Oh, I see. Sorry I jumped down your throat. How many employees here altogether?"

"Let's see. Besides me there're four full-timers, plus one who only works part-time. So, counting me and the part-timer, there's a total of six of us."

Joe spent a few minutes questioning Delmond, specifically about the car and what, if any, relationship he had with Knox or LaCroix. Then, one-by-one, all the others (except for the part-time employee, who worked only Wednesdays through Fridays) entered the office and faced basically the same questions from Joe. One employee in particular caught Joe's attention. Bill Lovett had worked at the body shop for only about eight months. Of more possible interest, he volunteered that he had spent seven years in prison in Wisconsin for the attempted rape and murder of a neighbor. In addition, he had a solid alibi only up until noon on Friday.

"I wasn't feeling well and left work early, about noon when we stopped work for lunch. I went home, where I live alone, and basically stayed in bed through most of Sunday. Must have been one of those 24-hour flus."

"No one saw you? Or spoke to you on the phone?"

"Nope. No one. I'm fairly new here, and I don't have many friends yet."

"I understand, Mr. Lovett. Why don't you give me your

home address? And phone number. We may have more questions as we get further into this case."

"Sure. No problem," said Lovett. He gave the information to Joe.

After a little over 90 minutes, Joe thanked Delmond and drove back to the station. He called Ginny from the parking lot. She was outside five minutes later, and the two of them walked around the corner to Sancho's for lunch.

CHAPTER 6

O ver lunch, Joe filled Ginny in on his visit to the auto body shop, focusing on how all the employees had access to the car and car keys, his interest in the ex-con, Lovett, and the need to go back and interview the part-time employee later in the week.

Ginny then brought Joe up to speed about her digging into LaCroix's history.

"Everything he said earlier about his marriage and divorce with Knox checked out. Plus, I picked up a few other interesting tidbits."

"Oh, I just love your tidbits. Let's have 'em."

"Seems like he's a pretty good guy. Except for a big anger-management problem."

"That's a pretty big 'except for.'"

"Sure is. Turns out he was suspended from college for a semester for getting into a fight with his roommate. Wound up breaking the roommate's nose and arm."

"Sounds like a full-scale brawl."

"Yeah. Seems that while he and his girlfriend, this is before Knox, were temporarily not seeing each other because of some fight about something, LaCroix's roommate took the girlfriend out on a date. Apparently, LaCroix went off the wall. Campus police had to be called to break up the fight. In the end, the roommate didn't press charges. As I said, the college suspended LaCroix for a semester.

"A few years later, when he and Knox were already together, he got into another slugfest, this time with their landlord. Seems LaCroix got pissed at how long it was taking the landlord to get LaCroix's leaky sink fixed. LaCroix was arrested, but wound up only having to attend an anger-management program."

"A leaky sink. Definitely something worth fighting about."

"And, of course, we already know about the 9-1-1 calls from Knox."

"As you said, Ginny, a great guy except for dot-dot-dot."

"Yup. He, along with your auto body shop ex-con, are clearly at the top of our suspect list so far."

"Full agreement, Partner."

Joe and Ginny spent part of the afternoon at their desks. They worked on checking the backgrounds, rap sheets, and Google-mentions for the manager and each of the employees at the auto body shop. Only Lovett came up with a criminal history, his prison stint for attempted rape and murder.

Around three o'clock, Ginny said, "OK, we can't postpone it any longer. Despite the cold, crappy weather, we need to interview the vic's neighbors. Maybe they saw or heard something. Or at least they can help us better understand her and what was going on in her life."

"Wish I had a good reason to disagree with you. But I don't. So, let's get going. It's only gonna get colder and nastier the later we're out there."

Joe and Ginny grabbed their hats and coats, stopped in the restrooms and were soon in Ginny's car on the way over to Knox's place.

Ginny parked in the street, directly in front of the victim's house.

Barely even looking at the house, Joe said, "OK, Ginny, left or right? Let's get through this before frostbite sets in."

"On my way. I'll head left. See you back here in an hour or two. First one back starts the motor and cranks up the heat."

"OK. Good luck."

Joe walked to the house on the right side of Knox's and rang the doorbell. The door opened and an attractive woman, probably in her early 40s, answered the door.

"Yes, can I help you?"

"Good afternoon. I'm Detective McFarland with the JC police," said Joe as he showed the woman his badge and ID. "I'd like to speak with you about your next-door neighbor, Ms. Knox."

"Yes, of course. Please come in. I'm Mary Thompson."

Joe followed her into the house. They both walked through the entranceway and took seats opposite each other in the living room.

"What a shame. Who would want to kill Kathryn? We've been sick since we heard."

"We're trying to find out who did it and why. What can you tell us about Ms. Knox?"

"Like what?"

"What kind of person she was. How well you knew her. Did she have any recent problems or worries? Did she seem to be acting differently lately? Any men in her life? The more we know about her, the better chance we have of developing and following the right trail."

"Well, let's see. We, that's my husband and I, have known her for about four years. That's when she and her husband, Rick, moved in next door. The four of us became quite friendly, going out to dinner or an occasional movie every few weeks. But then things started getting weird."

"Weird. In what way?"

"Maybe 'uncomfortable' is a better word. There were often loud arguments. We also think he hit her a few times. Occasionally the police even got called."

"Yes, we're aware of that."

"So, it became very weird, or as I said, uncomfortable. There'd be a loud argument, sometimes lasting hours, and maybe the police. Then, two days later we're going out to dinner with them and they're all lovey-dovey with each other. Couldn't tell if they'd really made up or were putting on an act for us. We gradually stopped going out with them. I mean, we were still friendly whenever we saw them outside, but we didn't go out with them anymore. Then, of course, Rick moved out when they separated and got divorced."

"Yes, we heard it was a less-than-friendly divorce."

"My goodness, yes. They apparently fought over everything. Bear in mind this is just what we heard from Kathryn, so we could never be really sure how true it was or who was at fault."

"I understand. And how was Ms. Knox after the divorce?"

"Amazing. She must have been a super strong woman. Or maybe she just wanted him out of her life. She seemed as friendly and upbeat as before. Like nothing major, like a divorce, had happened in her life. She obviously kept the house, continued with her same job and so on. She joined us a few times for dinner, but you could tell that she felt uncomfortable, like a third wheel. I've read about how people react in different ways when a single or divorced or even widowed woman socializes with a couple. We were fine with it, but it was clear that she wasn't. No one ever said anything, but we just gradually stopped socializing together."

"Any men in her life after the divorce?"

"Not much. Seemed to have an occasional date, but I don't think anything serious. No man ever left his car there all night or anything like that. Not that I would nose around, but this is a small, quiet neighborhood, so you'd notice things like that."

"I understand. Anyone she had a fight with, other than her husband? Any thoughts as to who might have killed her?"

"No to both those questions. That's why we were so shocked when this happened."

"That's about it. Thank you for your time, Mrs. Thompson. Here's my card. Please call if you, or your husband, think of anything else that may be helpful to us. In cases like this, even the smallest details are often important."

"OK. We will."

They said their good-byes, and Joe was soon back out in the cold. He rang the bells at seven other houses and spoke with the man or woman, and in one case a couple, who lived in four of them. Much of what Thompson had told Joe was confirmed, but no new information was learned.

When he got back to Ginny's car, Ginny was already in it, writing in her notepad while the heater pumped warm air throughout the cabin.

"Brrr, it's freezing out there," said Joe.

"Tell me about it."

"The heater feels fantastic, though."

While Joe and Ginny headed back to Joe's house for the night, Joe filled Ginny in on his interviews. Ginny then did the same. Much like Joe's, her interviews confirmed what they knew but added nothing else.

After dinner, they spent a few minutes discussing the new, recently-developed stage of their relationship.

"Ginny, I still can't believe that the chief knows about our personal situation and is allowing us to remain partners."

"No question, he sure is a tough one to predict. Not that I'm complaining in this case. Heck, just being able to go to a local restaurant or supermarket together without worrying about being seen is a load off our minds."

"Now we can start really planning our future together."

"Agreed. But one thing before we get to that."

"Uh oh. What?"

"Don't panic, Joe. I just want us to remember that the chief put a few conditions on his ongoing approval."

"Yeah, I know. But they're not so tough to adhere to."

"We've been good about not being overly romantic in the office, but we've not really done much to include some of the guys when we get coffee for each other, or go out to lunch."

"Ginny, I got coffee for Jones twice last week. And we invited Caruso and Klein to lunch. It's not our fault they had that early afternoon meeting in Columbus and had to pass."

"I know. We've done a little. But we haven't yet made it a part of our natural work routine. It's like a major planned event whenever we try to involve our co-workers."

"That's normal, Ginny. After all the time we spent being careful to keep our relationship secret, it'll take a while for us to get used to being more open and inviting."

"I know. I just don't want us to forget. We can't let our sloppiness or forgetfulness or whatever it is mess up the great deal we have going right now."

"Full agreement. Let's both try to remember this more often. But now, let's talk about our future."

"OK. Like what?"

"Well, to start with, what are we, Ginny?"

"Huh? Whaddaya mean?"

"I mean are we friends, part-time roommates, boy-friend and girlfriend, fiancé and fiancée, or what?"

"Good question. Right now, I think we're boyfriend and girlfriend. We only move to the next level if and when we definitely decide to get married."

"And what about where we live? Right now, we have my house and your condo, even though we spend almost every night together. You said if we move into a house together, it should be one that we jointly buy as *our* house. Not my existing house. And not your condo, which is too small anyhow. I get that. Should we start house hunting now?"

"Maybe the place to start is just with the two of us. We should try to describe what we'd want. Type of house, its size, layout, location. And, of course, the price."

"Also, how old it is. What materials it's made of, and how big a garage it has. And the size of the property, and what the neighborhood's like."

"All good points. Then we could initially look online, just to get a sense of whether what we're looking for exists. And at a halfway reasonable price."

"Ginny, are you hesitant to move ahead?"

"No, Joe! Not at all." Then, after a few seconds, "Uh, well, in fact, maybe a little."

"Oh?"

"No, Joe. It's not what you think. It's just . . . the house thing. We occasionally both enjoy being in our own place, alone. Will we miss that? Will we start to feel trapped with just one house?"

"Spoken like a true real estate mogul. But seriously, I understand what you're saying. Maybe it means we need the house to have a spare bedroom, or a man cave for me or a separate sitting room for you. And what about the marriage thing?"

"Joe, there's no question, none, that I want to spend the rest of my life with you. But I'm deathly afraid of pushing you to move too fast, before you're one hundred percent ready."

"Why don't you think I'm ready right now?"

"Joe, I know how you still feel about Lori. And Adam. And I respect that. You've come a long way in not feeling as guilty, like being with me is cheating on Lori. These things take time to fade away. I don't expect or want you to stop remembering them, but I want to be sure that if we do get married, you won't start feeling guilty about it."

"Ginny, I—"

"Joe, no need to try to explain it. I understand. I really do."

"You're amazing, Ginny."

"You're not too bad yourself."

"OK, let's quit for now. Agreeing that we're both fantastic is a good place to stop."

"Fair enough. I'm ready for bed anyhow."

"Ditto."

CHAPTER 7

"**O**K, Ginny. I'm going to get us some coffee."

"Thanks."

"Hey, Vern. Steve. Want some coffee?"

"Yeah, sure. Thanks, Joe," said Steve Klein.

"No, thanks, Joe. I'm on my way to the courthouse," said Vern Jones.

"Jeez, I hope they find you not guilty," said Klein.

Joe returned carrying three cups of black coffee, with Klein's loaded up with three spoonfuls of sugar, just the way he liked it.

"Thanks, Joe."

"My pleasure."

Giving Ginny her cup, Joe sat down and said, "OK. I think we should go visit the vic's company today."

"Yup. Let's see what her boss can tell us."

"I'll make an appointment with him for this morning, if I can."

"OK. And we should also talk with her assistant. They usually know more about what's going on than anyone."

Joe called to make an appointment with Philip Van Hale, the president. His executive assistant scheduled the meeting for 10:30.

A few minutes later, Ginny's phone rang.

"Good morning. This is Detective Harris."

"Hello, Detective. Uh…"

"Yes? Who is this? How can I help you?"

"This is Shaun Knox. I'm calling from Marlboro, Massachusetts."

"Yes, hello, Mr. Knox. We're so sorry about your daughter."

"That's why we're calling. Do you know what happened? Who did it? And why?"

"We're in the process of trying to figure all that out. My partner and I, and several of our colleagues, are totally focused on this."

"When can we bring our baby back home?"

"You mean to Marlboro?"

"Yes. We have a family plot in the local cemetery, and that's where Katie belongs. Her career took her to so many different places, but none of them are really home for her. This is the only home she ever had."

"I'm not sure, Mr. Knox, but I think the medical examiner still needs two or three days to finish his work."

"That'll be OK. We're thinking of getting to Jasper Creek on Thursday. That'll give us a day or two to go through all her things at her house, and figure out what to take home and what to give or throw away. And we'll need to find a real estate agent to work on selling her house. So, we can keep busy until she's ready to fly home with us."

"That makes sense. Mr. Knox, I think it would be simplest for you if you had your local funeral director call me, and I'll put him in touch with the medical examiner here. They can then work out the details among themselves."

"OK, I'll do that. And Nancy, that's my wife, and I will stop in to see you once we're there."

"Excellent. We look forward to seeing you on Thursday. And again, our most sincere sympathies."

Ginny filled Joe in on the call.

"Bummer. It's never easy when a family member dies, but when it's your child it's super tough. A child dying before the parents just isn't the normal order of things."

Although he didn't mention the death of his own son, Ginny couldn't help thinking of it. *The poor guy went through hell and back. It's amazing he made it through. Shows how strong he is.*

"OK, let's get going, or we'll be late for our appointment at National Pipe."

"Right behind you, Joe."

Joe parked in National Pipe's visitors parking area at 10:20. He and Ginny walked through the front doors into a two-story, fairly modern steel-and-glass administration building that clearly had been added onto the old, three-story red brick manufacturing building attached to it. They spoke with the receptionist, who called Van Hale's office.

"Detectives, have a seat please. Mr. Van Hale's executive assistant will be right down."

Five minutes later, an attractive 30ish-year-old woman entered the lobby. Tall and thin, she appeared even more so in her three-inch high-heeled shoes. Smiling, she walked up to Joe and Ginny. "Good morning, Detectives. I'm Carol Nesbitt, Mr. Van Hale's executive assistant. Please come with me. I'll show you to his office."

"Thank you," said Ginny.

After following Nesbitt up one flight of stairs and down

a short hallway, they were at Van Hale's office. Nesbitt knocked on the door jamb as she simultaneously led Joe and Ginny into the office.

Van Hale stood up and walked around to the front of his desk. Just under six feet tall, with dark hair, except for some graying at the temples, and what appeared to be an athletic body, Van Hale looked like he was straight out of central casting to play a senior executive. After introductions and "no thanks" to Nesbitt's offer of coffee, Nesbitt left, closing the door behind her. The three others sat down around a small conference table in one corner of the office.

"Mr. Van Hale," said Ginny, "we'd like to talk about Ms. Knox."

"Yes. Yes, of course. We still can't wrap our minds around it. Who would want to kill her? Such a sweet and talented woman. In the prime of her life."

"Mr. Van Hale, when did you last see Ms. Knox?"

"Friday afternoon. She worked until about six, and then left. Always so dedicated to the job. Often the last one to leave. Even on a Friday evening."

"Were you still here when she left?"

"Yes, I was here until a little past seven. But that's different — I'm the president. And owner of the company."

"Mr. Van Hale, did she seem different in any way the last few times you saw her? Upset or worried? Or scared?"

"No, she seemed perfectly normal. She was always upbeat and smiling. Always cheered up a room when she walked in."

"Was she having any difficulties with anyone at work?" asked Joe.

"No. I mean, as CFO she often had to say 'no' to someone's request, or push someone to cut costs or perform better. But people understood that was her job. I don't recall her ever having a personal problem with anyone here."

"What about with her ex-husband?"

"Well, yes. But that was a unique situation. It was apparently a less-than-friendly divorce, although I never got into any of the details with her. In any event, Rick, that's Rick LaCroix, her ex-husband, left here soon after the divorce."

"Did you fire him?"

"What? No. Although we hired him as part of our hiring Kathryn, it was a real hire. We needed that quality assurance role filled, and Rick was fully qualified for it. In fact, he did a very good job for us while he was here. He quit totally on his own. He was very upset about Kathryn divorcing him, and he said it was too painful for him to work here and see her every day."

"Any idea who might want her dead? Or why?"

"No. None at all."

"Mr. Van Hale," said Ginny. "Any idea where Ms. Knox's car is? We can't seem to locate it."

"That's weird. It would normally be at her house, unless she went someplace . . . and that's where the murderer grabbed her."

"When we spoke the other day, you gave us a full description of her car except for the full plate number."

"I'll ask Ms. Nesbitt to get it for you."

"Thank you. And thank you for your time," said Ginny. "We may be back if we have more questions. Here are our cards if you think of anything else." After Joe and Ginny handed him their cards, Ginny continued, "Now, Mr. Van Hale, we'd like to take a look at Ms. Knox's office and computer and meet with her assistant, as well as some of her co-workers and subordinates."

"You already have."

"Excuse me?"

"Met her executive assistant. Ms. Nesbitt, my executive assistant, is, or was, also Kathryn's. We're a small enough company that we have to do a lot of cost-saving things like that."

"Oh, we didn't realize. Perhaps we can speak with her now, and then she can show us to Ms. Knox's office and introduce us to some of the others."

"Sure. Let's walk over to Ms. Nesbitt's desk."

The three of them exited Van Hale's office and stopped at Nesbitt's desk right outside his office door.

"Carol, these detectives would like to talk with you for a few minutes, and then they'd like to go through Kathryn's office. They'd also like you to introduce them to some of her co-workers and subordinates. Oh, and while they're looking through Kathryn's office, please get the license plate of Kathryn's car for them."

"No problem, Mr. Van Hale. Detectives, let's go sit in Ms. Knox's office. Then, after we're done speaking, I'll leave so you can go through everything."

"Excellent. Thanks," said Ginny.

Two minutes later, they were sitting at a round conference table in Knox's former office.

"Detectives, do you have any idea who killed Kathryn? I still can't believe it."

"Not yet," said Ginny. "We're only in the early stages of our investigation. Do you have any thoughts about who might have wanted her dead?"

"No. Not at all. She was liked and respected by everyone. I can't think of anyone. If this was right after her divorce about two years ago, I might have suspected her husband, but not now."

"Why would you have suspected him?" asked Joe.

"It was a pretty unfriendly divorce. And Mr. LaCroix was very upset. In fact, he left the company just to be away from her."

"When did you last see her?" asked Ginny.

"Friday, about five in the afternoon. I left around then, and she was still in her office working."

"Ms. Nesbitt, did Ms. Knox seem upset or worried about anything in the few days prior to her death?"

"Not that I could see. She seemed perfectly normal."

"After her divorce, did she date much? Was she involved with anyone else?"

"Well, at first she didn't date or anything. Then gradually, she started going on occasional dates. But I don't think it was anything serious. Until . . . ."

"Until when? And what?" prompted Ginny.

"It's nothing I can put my finger on. Kathryn was always very private about her personal life. But starting, oh, I don't know, maybe nine or ten months ago, it seemed like she was more seriously involved with someone."

"Who?" asked Joe.

"I have no idea. Like I said, she was very private. She started closing her door for certain phone calls. And she left early on a number of Fridays. At first, I thought maybe she was looking for another job. But I came to think, or *feel* might be more accurate, that it was a man."

"And you have no idea who?"

"Nope. None."

"OK, thanks, Ms. Nesbitt. Here are our cards if you think of anything else. Now, you can leave us here. We want to rummage through her office and computer. Do we need a password for her laptop?"

"Yes. But it's a pretty simple one: Knox321$."

"OK. Thanks."

"You're welcome. Sure hope you catch whoever did this."

"We'll be doing our very best. We'll let you know when we're done here. Then you can bring in some of the others, one at a time, for us to talk with."

Nesbitt left and closed the door. Joe and Ginny got to work. Ginny sat down in front of the laptop, entered the password Nesbitt had provided and started searching through files, e-mails and the Outlook calendar. Joe did the physical search of files, desk drawers and bookcases.

Joe and Ginny spent about 45 minutes searching through Knox's office and laptop, but didn't find much. About the only thing of interest was Ginny's observation from browsing through Knox's Outlook calendar.

"Joe, nothing definitive, but I may have spotted something interesting."

"What is it?"

"Up until last spring, her calendar was solid meetings, almost from dawn to dusk."

"And?"

"Then, starting April or so of last year, her meetings

often began a little later in the morning. And ended earlier in the afternoon. First, about once a week, and gradually increasing to roughly three days per week."

"You mean like she was spending more evenings and early mornings with her secret boyfriend?"

"Yeah. Unless she was spending all that time at a gym or yoga studio. No appointments for these times were on her calendar. While we're at it, I'm going to have Forensics go through this laptop. Maybe there's some hidden stuff that I can't see."

"Good idea. Let's tell Ms. Nesbitt we're ready to meet the others. After that, it'll be time for a lunch break. You can call about the laptop along the way."

Joe and Ginny returned to Nesbitt. They explained that they were finished in Knox's office, but that their colleagues would be along to borrow Knox's laptop. They asked Nesbitt to call them once the funeral arrangements were set. Nesbitt said she would. She also gave them Knox's license plate number: NP 443.

Nesbitt then started bringing others in, one at a time. Joe and Ginny spoke with three of Knox's fellow executives and four of her subordinates, but they didn't learn anything or get any suspicious feelings. They then went back to Nesbitt's desk. She escorted them down to the lobby, where they said their good-byes.

A quick stop at a pizza parlor, after which Joe drove back to the station.

While Joe was driving, Ginny called the desk sergeant, giving him the three numbers of Knox's license plate and asking him to update the state-wide BOLO with the full plate number. She then called Forensics and asked them to pick up and examine Knox's laptop at National Pipe, and to be sure to also check the laptop that the Crime Scene technicians had picked up at Knox's house.

CHAPTER 8

Back at their desks, Joe and Ginny knocked out some of the paperwork on two now-closed cases that they had been avoiding for over a week. Two hours later, just as they were cleaning up their desks and getting ready to head home, Ginny received a call from the desk sergeant downstairs.

"Hi, Ginny. This must be your lucky day."

"Why's that, Sarge? 'Cause I get to speak to you twice today?"

"Yeah, there's that, too. But I was referring to the fact that we got a hit on your BOLO."

"Wow. Really? That's quick."

"Sure is. A uniform over in Lennox found it parked in a shopping center."

"Great. Gimme the details."

After getting the details and hanging up, Ginny told Joe what she had just learned.

"That's a lucky break. Let's head over there now. We can have a couple of the Crime Scene guys meet us. Let's also see if the Lennox patrolman who spotted the car can meet us there."

While Joe drove, Ginny called the Crime Scene Department and then the Lennox Police Department to see if the Crime Scene technicians and the Lennox officer could meet them at the shopping center.

Fifteen minutes later, Joe pulled into the shopping

center parking lot. With a patrol car directly behind it, it was easy to spot Knox's car. Joe drove over and stopped behind the patrol car. A brief discussion with the officer provided no useful information. He had been making his typical drive through the parking lot and was approaching where the car was parked when the BOLO update came through his radio. Talk about timing. But he could offer no specific information about how long the car had been there. He did point out, however, that the relatively small amount of snow under the car, along with the snowplow tracks around the car, indicated that the car had been parked there before the heavy snow. As the patrolman was leaving, two Crime Scene technicians arrived. They checked out the surrounding area, picking up and bagging all sorts of nothings they found lying on the ground. Then they called one of the Jasper Creek towing companies they used to come get the car and take it back to the Forensics lab.

Joe and Ginny started checking each of the shops in the shopping center, except for the few that had already closed for the day, to see if anyone recognized Knox from the picture they showed. No success at the tanning salon, 7-Eleven convenience store, 24/7 gym, ladies' clothing shop or popcorn store. But they were successful at La Pentola, an upscale Italian restaurant near one end of the shopping center.

"Yes, she's been in here," said the manager. "Several times, in fact. Always for dinner."

"Alone?"

"No. Always with a man. Sometimes he comes in with her. Other times, they meet here."

"Do you know his name? Do they usually charge their meal?"

"Sorry, no to both questions. I never heard either of their names. And there are no credit card receipts to check. They always pay cash."

"Can you describe the man?"

"A little bit. About five-foot-ten, not fat or thin, dark hair."

"How old? Any distinctive features, or marks or scars?"

"I'm not good at ages, but I'd say early 50s. And nothing distinctive."

"When were they last here?"

"Not sure. All the days blur together. But Rosa may know."

"Rosa?"

"The waitress who usually takes care of them. They never make reservations, but whenever they come, they prefer to sit in Rosa's area if there's an available table."

"OK. May we speak with her?"

"Sure. Let me get her."

A brief discussion with Rosa confirmed everything the manager had told Joe and Ginny.

"Rosa," Ginny said, "we're trying to determine when the woman was last in here."

"It was either last Thursday or Friday evening."

"How can you be so sure?" asked Joe.

"Easy. We're closed Mondays, I was out sick Tuesday and Wednesday, and they never come in on Saturday or Sunday."

"That makes sense."

"I know they were in recently, like last week, but I can't remember if it was Thursday or Friday."

Joe and Ginny questioned her about the description of Knox's male companion, but Rosa was just about as vague as the manager had been.

"Not a problem," said Joe. "You've been very helpful. We may be back if we have more questions. And perhaps with photos, to see if you can identify her companion."

"Fine."

Joe and Ginny thanked Rosa and the manager, and headed back to their car. Checking the parking lot, they were pleased to see several video cameras. They found the small office of the shopping center's manager in one corner of the row of shops, but it was locked tight. Ginny copied the name and phone number on the door into her notebook.

"Joe, looks like the vic definitely had a new guy in her life."

"Yeah. And they were going out of their way to keep it a secret."

"Just like we did, until the chief gave us the all clear."

"Exactly. But now we have to somehow figure out who lover boy is."

"Yup. Too bad his description sounds like half of all adult males."

"That waitress," said Joe, "had a logical way of narrowing it down to last Thursday or Friday evening. When we have our suspects lined up, we should return here with photos. Or, if need be, get her and the sketch artist together."

"Definitely. And it would be nice to know which night.

Friday would clearly move the secret dinner companion to the very top of our suspect list."

"For sure. Also, that restaurant looked pretty nice. We should put it on our to-try list."

"Agreed. But, Joe, let's solve the case first."

"Deal. Let's plan on our celebration dinner here after we solve it."

"Works for me," said Ginny as they got into Joe's car and headed back to Jasper Creek.

CHAPTER 9

The next morning, Ginny drove to the station while Joe drove to Sunshine Auto.

"Good morning, Detective," said Delmond, the body shop manager. "Back so soon? How can I help you today?"

"Morning. I want to spend a few minutes with your part-time employee."

"Oh, yeah. That's right. I forgot. You can stay here in my office, I'll go get him for you."

A few minutes later, Delmond walked back into his office with another fellow behind him. "Detective, this is Tom Parsons. He's our part-timer, who you missed the other day. You two can stay right here. I need to be out on the floor for a while anyways."

"OK, thanks." Then, turning to Parsons, Joe introduced himself. Both he and Parson sat down. Fifteen minutes later, Joe was finished. Parsons was fairly new to the area, having moved to Jasper Creek less than five months ago. He also had what sounded like a solid alibi. He had worked all day Friday, then right from work drove the ten-plus hours to his hometown in Kansas for the weekend and early part of the week. Joe got a few names and phone numbers of people he could check with in Kansas, and headed to the station.

Once back at his desk, Joe called the names in Kansas.

They confirmed Parsons' arrival and departure times, essentially eliminating him as a suspect in Knox's murder.

While Joe had been at the body shop, Ginny tracked down the manager of the shopping center where La Pentola was located. Confirming that they had the recordings from video cameras in the parking lot, Ginny made an 11 o'clock appointment for her and Joe to view the videos.

Joe and Ginny were in the shopping center manager's office at 10:45, and viewing the videos by 11. Sure enough, on the recording of the prior Friday evening, they clearly saw Knox drive up and park at 7:15 PM. She sat in her car for about five minutes, getting out only when a man walked up to her car. Knox got out of her car and locked it, then stretched up and kissed the man. Hand-in-hand, they then walked in the direction of the restaurant. Unfortunately, the camera only caught the man from behind. Judging from his standing next to Knox, he was probably about six feet tall. With his hat and overcoat on, nothing else could be seen or estimated. Joe and Ginny checked all the other camera recordings, but didn't see anyone who might be the mystery man. The view of the man was so limited, Joe and Ginny agreed that there was no point in having Rosa look at the video. They also never saw Knox or her hatted and overcoated companion leaving the restaurant or parking lot. Knox obviously left her car sitting in the lot, and both of them most likely walked to her companion's car, unfortunately not captured by video.

"Well, Joe. This is no help in identifying lover boy, but

at least it confirms the time that he and the vic went into the restaurant Friday night."

"Yeah. If they were walking in just before 7:30, I'd guess they probably left the restaurant sometime between 8:30 and 9:30."

"Sounds reasonable to me. Having dinner there'd take a bit longer than it takes us to normally wolf down a pizza and beer."

"Right about that. Well, at least we've got the start of a timeline. She clearly wasn't killed before Friday evening."

"Yup. This nicely narrows the time span estimate from the ME."

"Speaking about wolfing down a pizza, let's head back to the station and find a pizza joint along the way."

"Works for me, Joe."

Following lunch, Joe and Ginny were back at their desks at the station.

"Joe, how tall do you think that ex-con at the body shop is? Also, what's your guess about LaCroix?"

"Hmm. Let me think for a sec.

"Unfortunately, I'd bet they're both similar in height to that guy in the video. Good try, but we can't eliminate either of them based on our height estimating."

"Well, they're still our two hot suspects at the moment. Should we bring 'em both in?"

"Yup. I think so. Let's go get LaCroix, and then Lovett."

"Works for me. As a minimum, we'll work off our aggression and frustration."

Just then, Ginny got a call from Forensics. They confirmed that there were no hidden or encrypted files on either Knox's work or home laptop.

"Too bad. But we appreciate you guys checking. And your speed."

"Here to please," responded the tech.

Ginny filled Joe in on the call.

"Too bad. But not surprising. Guess we still have to work the case the old-fashioned way."

Joe checked with Van Hale at National Pipe to find out where LaCroix went to work after his resignation. An hour later, Joe and Ginny were in the lobby at Precision Components, waiting for LaCroix, whom the receptionist had called.

As he walked into the lobby, LaCroix said, "Hello, Detectives. Any news on Kathryn's death?"

"Yes, we believe so," said Ginny.

"Great, what did you learn?"

"We learned that we need to take you back to the station for some more questions."

"What? Do you think—?"

"We'll do the asking," said Joe. "I'll walk you back to your office so you can get your coat."

LaCroix walked back to his office, with Joe following right behind him. He grabbed his hat and coat, and told his secretary that he had to go out for a meeting.

A half-hour later, Joe, Ginny and LaCroix were sitting in one of the interrogation rooms at headquarters.

Joe turned his recorder on and stated the date, time and who was present. He then read LaCroix his Miranda rights.

"As soon as this foolishness develops too far, I'm going to stop answering questions and call my attorney."

"No problem," said Ginny. "That's your right."

"Let's go through things again. Where were you last Friday night and early Saturday morning?" asked Joe.

"Like I told you the first time, I was home Friday night. Susie and I stayed home watching TV. We had no place special to go, and, as you may recall, the weather sucked."

"What time did you get home that evening?"

"About 5:30 or so. Susie was already home because her company shut down production early."

"And where were you Saturday morning?" asked Ginny.

"Also home. Susie took my car to the supermarket. I assume you haven't forgotten that. So I couldn't have gone anywhere even if I wanted to."

"Tell us more about your divorce from Ms. Knox," said Joe.

"What do you want to know?"

"It was a pretty unfriendly split. Wasn't it?"

"Yeah. I told you that last time."

"What was the divorce about?" asked Ginny.

"Damned if I know. Like I also told you, she just walked out one day. No forewarning. No explanation."

"Think your repeated beatings of her might have played a role?" asked Ginny.

"What beatings?"

"Mr. LaCroix, we're not as ignorant as you must think. We know about the calls to 9-1-1."

"Yeah, but there were never any charges filed. Doesn't that count for anything?"

"Not much," said Joe. "You also have an earlier history

of fighting. Looks like real anger-management issues to me."

"Well, not to me. Anyhow, if I was going to kill her, why would I wait until two years after our divorce?"

"No idea. Why don't you tell us? Maybe it took you that long to get up the guts to do it."

"That's it. I'm done. I'm either leaving or calling my lawyer. Which should it be?"

"You're free to leave, Mr. LaCroix. In fact, we'll walk you downstairs and arrange for one of our uniformed officers to take you back to work. Here are our cards. Be sure to contact one of us before you leave the state."

"Yeah. Sure."

Joe and Ginny gave him their cards, and Ginny escorted him downstairs.

Back upstairs, Ginny said, "Boy, what a bum."

"Full agreement there. But, so far, all we've got is that we don't like him. That's probably just a bit shy of what we need for a conviction."

"Just a bit. You want to go get that Lovett fellow from the body shop, and we'll see what we can squeeze out of him."

"You bet. I'll be back shortly," said Joe as he grabbed his coat and headed to his car.

Forty-five minutes later, Joe, Ginny and Lovett were sitting in the same interrogation room Joe and Ginny had used earlier with LaCroix.

"Let me ask you again — why're you picking on me? I'm sure I'm not the only one without an airtight alibi."

"Not only isn't yours airtight, it doesn't even have a lid on it," said Joe.

"Very cute."

"Mr. Lovett," said Ginny, "we're not picking on you. We're trying to solve a murder."

"I get that. But why would I kill her? Hell, I never even met the lady."

"Oh, you mean not like the neighbor, who you knew?" said Joe.

"What do you—"

"You know exactly what we mean," said Joe. "Your neighbor in Wisconsin. And your attempted-rape-and-murder conviction."

"That was a long time ago. And I'm the one who told you about it."

"Right. Like we wouldn't have quickly found out about it, even if you hadn't told me."

"Do I need a lawyer?"

"Up to you," said Ginny. "You heard your rights. Most guilty people would call for a lawyer about now."

"What happened?" asked Joe. "You wanted to have sex with Ms. Knox, but she said no. So an attempted rape got out of control and you killed her. Hell, maybe it was an accident. Tell us what happened. We might be able to help you."

"Yeah. I can just picture how helpful you'd be."

"All right, Lovett. Enough of this BS now. Tell us exactly when you conveniently got sick that Friday. And where you were and what you did, from then until early Saturday morning."

"I told you the first time we met. I got sick on Friday, went home at lunch time and stayed there all day Saturday and most of Sunday."

"No one saw you? You didn't have to buy some food? Or go to the pharmacy for some medicine? Or go to the lobby to get your mail?"

"No. I just stayed home, in bed almost the whole time."

"Well, that makes you very unlucky, Mr. Lovett. You're now number one on our hit parade of suspects."

"Yeah. Well, I didn't do it. And you'll need some evidence to prove that I did. Just having no alibi and being an ex-con aren't evidence."

"You are correct. We don't have hard evidence yet. And note my emphasis on the word *yet*."

"OK, Sir. You're free to go," said Ginny. Following the standard warning about not leaving the state without contacting them first, Ginny walked Lovett downstairs and arranged for a ride back to work for him.

Back upstairs, Ginny said, "I don't know, Joe. I could like either of them for it. But if I had to place my bet now, I'd put my money on LaCroix."

"I agree. Can't say why, but that's what my gut's saying also."

"Nice to know that our guts are so perfectly aligned," said Ginny with a smile.

"OK. Time to call it a day. Let's head over to my place, grab a quick dinner, catch some TV and then work on tightly aligning our guts."

"Works for me."

Just before they left the station, Ginny got a phone call.

"Joe, that was Carol Nesbitt, the vic's executive assistant. The funeral is scheduled for Friday morning. Services at nine at St. John's, followed by the burial out at Pine Lawn."

"Well, as usual, we'll attend. Never know what or who we'll see. Or hear."

"Roger that, Partner," said Ginny as she and Joe headed for the parking lot.

CHAPTER 10

First thing next morning, Ginny stopped in to see the Patrol sergeant. The uniforms canvassing LaCroix's neighbors, as well as Knox's neighbors, had come up with big fat nothings. No one had seen or heard anything even slightly out of the ordinary. Everyone's windows had been sealed tight against the wintery weather.

"Joe, what say we take another shot at LaCroix's girlfriend? I think we've got a decent chance of getting her to tell us more than she has if we get to her while LaCroix's at work. If she's holding something back, our good cop/bad cop routine might shake something loose."

"Good idea. Let's head over to National Pipe and bring her back here."

Once again, Joe and Ginny were back in the interrogation room. Ginny stated the when, who and where into the tape recorder and read Ray her rights.

"Yeah. I understand all that. But why'd you read it to me? Am I a suspect?"

"Ms. Ray, we read them to everyone we speak with here at the station. It's just a precaution."

"OK. Now, what is it that you couldn't ask me at the plant, but had to drag me all the way over here for?"

"Going back to last Friday, what time did you get home from work?"

"Umm. Let's see. It was about 3:30. They shut down early 'cause of the snowstorm moving in."

"And was your boyfriend home when you got home?"

"No. In fact, we teased each other the next day. His company didn't shut down early at all because of the weather forecast. I said they were cold-hearted. He said their employees weren't all wimps, like where I worked."

"What time did he get home that evening?"

"About eleven or so."

"Oh, that late?"

"Yeah. But he called me about five. He explained that they were trying to finish a couple of large orders. And, since there'd probably be no overtime for the plant on Saturday because of the snow, they decided to stay late Friday and finish the work. And, of course, he had to be there to sign off on the quality when they finished."

"And when he got home?" asked Joe.

"Late as it was, and even as tired as he was, he started shoveling the driveway. But, he only got about half, maybe a little less, of it done and gave up for the night. You saw how the driveway was only half cleared."

"Yes, we did," said Ginny.

"And that's why I took his car to the supermarket on Saturday morning. And you know the rest after that."

"Yes, we surely do," said Joe, in his most somber voice.

"Why do you say it like that?"

"Because we think your boyfriend, and perhaps also you, know more than you've told us so far."

"Like what?"

"Like why Ms. Knox was killed. And why she was put in your boyfriend's car trunk. And who did it."

"How would he, or I, know any of that?"

"By being involved."

"No way. What are you saying?"

"Ms. Ray, would you be concerned if you learned that your boyfriend told us he was home with you that whole Friday evening?"

"I don't believe it. You must have misunderstood him. He wouldn't lie about something like that."

"Ms. Ray, I'll be right back," said Joe. "I'm going to get the recording of our discussion with him yesterday."

Joe left and returned a few minutes later.

"Ms. Ray, here's part of our session with your boyfriend. You tell us if we misunderstood him."

Joe played the recording, fast-forwarding to the section where LaCroix said he was home from 5:30 on that evening.

"I think I understood it correctly. What do you think?"

"My God. There must be some mistake. I'm sure that Rick can explain this."

"Don't be too sure," offered Ginny.

Joe and Ginny stepped into the hall, leaving Ray sitting at the small table in the interrogation room.

"Joe, I think we've got him. Might not be enough yet for a conviction, but I bet it's enough for an arrest warrant."

"I agree, Ginny. And an arrest might be enough to scare the whole truth out of him. Why don't you babysit her while I call the prosecutor's office and see if they can hustle up a warrant?"

"Will do. Good luck."

"Thanks."

Ginny went back into the room while Joe walked to

his desk and called Charles Porter, the county prosecutor. Porter was in court, so Joe was connected to Donna Gantz, one of the assistant prosecuting attorneys.

"Hello. APA Gantz."

"Hi. This is Detective McFarland over at JCPD. I don't think we've met before."

"No, I don't think so either. I'm fairly new here. How can I help you?"

"Looking for an arrest warrant."

"Fill me in."

"We've got a hot suspect for the murder of Kathryn Knox. The one found in the trunk of that car last Saturday morning."

"Ugh. Gross. I don't even like to think about it."

"Turns out the owner of the car is her ex. Several 9-1-1 calls during their marriage. He's got a history of anger management issues. Also caught him lying to us about his alibi during part of the time span estimated for the murder."

"Based on what you've described, we can probably get the warrant. But just between you and me, it sounds like you're coming up way short of enough for a conviction."

"Well aware of that. We want to arrest him, even briefly. To scare the heck out of him as a minimum. Might get him to start talking."

"Understood. But, as I'm sure you know, we're not fond of getting warrants when we don't think we have enough for a reasonable chance of a conviction. I'll need to pass this by Mr. Porter first."

"OK. Hopefully that won't cause a big delay."

"Shouldn't. I think I'll have an answer for you within

an hour, two hours tops. Seems like the judge calls for breaks every hour or so. Maybe he's got a weak bladder. What's your phone number?"

Joe gave Gantz his phone number, thanked her and hung up.

Joe called Ginny out of the interrogation room and filled her in.

Sure enough, a little more than an hour later, Gantz called Joe to inform him that she'd just got the arrest warrant for LaCroix and was faxing it to Joe.

Ginny arranged for one of the other detectives to wait 45 minutes and then tell Ray she was free to leave, take her downstairs and arrange for a patrol car to drive her back to work. This 45 minutes would give Ginny and Joe time to get to LaCroix before Ray could call and alert him to the discrepancy in their Friday night descriptions.

Slightly after noon, Joe and Ginny entered the employee cafeteria at Precision Components and very publicly arrested LaCroix for the murder of Kathryn Knox. All eyes remained focused on the events playing out, as Ginny handcuffed LaCroix's hands behind his back and Ginny and Joe marched him out of the cafeteria, his mostly-un-eaten lunch left on the table. LaCroix was embarrassed and furious, but couldn't do anything about it.

Back in the same interrogation room, Ginny went through the standard initial statements for the recording machine, and then read LaCroix his rights.

"Yeah, sure. I understand all that. But what's this for? How can you think I murdered Kathryn? Where's your evidence?"

"Mr. LaCroix," said Joe, "do you recall telling us that you got home from work about 5:30 on Friday evening?"

"Yeah. So?"

"Well, congratulations," said Joe.

"Huh? What do you mean?"

"You must be one great magician. To get home at 5:30 while, at the same time, not leaving work until after 10 that evening. Amazing. How'd you do that trick?"

"You got it wrong. Somebody's either confused or lied to you. I didn't work late that night."

"Mr. LaCroix, we've learned the truth from several sources. You did work late that evening, because the snowstorm wasn't going to allow overtime on Saturday to finish some important jobs. Most of the time you were alone in your office or the quality control lab, so no one can be sure you didn't sneak out for an hour or so."

"What a bunch of big mouths!"

"Is that all you can say? Why'd you lie to us?"

"Because I knew how it would look if I didn't have an airtight alibi. I know how you guys think."

"Well then," said Ginny, "you're surely aware that we think someone who lies to us about their alibi must be suspicious at best."

"Would you like to change your statement about Friday night?" asked Joe.

"Yeah. Sure. OK, I worked. Until almost 10:30, like you said, to sign off on some rush production work. Then I went straight home."

"And when did you leave work for a while that evening? And where'd you go?" asked Joe.

"No place. I didn't leave at all until I went home at 10:30."

"And who can confirm that?" asked Ginny.

"Not sure anyone can. I mean, a lot of people saw me, but not for the whole time. I was doing stuff in my office and in the lab several times while everyone else was working on the production floor."

"So, in other words, you don't have a solid alibi for the whole evening," said Ginny.

"Well, yeah. But it's true. And that's why I lied to you the first time. I knew you wouldn't believe me."

"That's the first thing you've gotten right. We don't believe you," said Joe.

"What about all that 'innocent until proven guilty' stuff?"

"That only applies to your trial. Not to your arrest," said Ginny.

"I think I want my lawyer now."

"Smart move," said Joe. "Go ahead and call him."

While waiting for LaCroix's lawyer to show up, Ginny arranged for one of the other detectives to bring back sandwiches and sodas for the three of them. Ginny gave LaCroix his lunch in the interrogation room, after which she and Joe went to their desks to eat theirs.

About two hours later, Vernon O'Hara, LaCroix's lawyer, arrived. After Joe and Ginny summarized the situation to O'Hara, and O'Hara unsuccessfully argued that his client not be arrested as the police had no hard evidence, Joe and Ginny took LaCroix for processing. O'Hara told LaCroix that he'd get him out, with little or no bail, the next day.

CHAPTER 11

The next morning, Joe and Ginny were sitting in Ginny's car across the street from the church where Knox's funeral was being held. There was quite a crowd attending. Joe and Ginny recognized Van Hale and Nesbitt, as well as a few of Knox's coworkers and subordinates whom they had interviewed. They knew LaCroix wouldn't be there because his bail hearing wasn't scheduled until later that morning. They assumed Knox's parents had arrived sometime the prior day and were at the funeral, but they couldn't identify which of the couples arriving for the funeral were them.

Just before nine, Joe and Ginny entered the church and sat in the last row of the almost-filled nave. Several people, including Van Hale, gave short eulogies. *Despite all these loving comments, there's obviously at least one person who doesn't agree,* Joe thought as he listened to the tributes. *All we have to do is find him or her.*

Joe and Ginny decided not to go to the cemetery. They preferred to watch the action, if any, at LaCroix's bail hearing.

Sure enough, at a short court hearing at eleven o'clock, the judge released LaCroix on his own recognizance without the need to post bail.

Walking back to the station from the courthouse, Ginny said, "Well, that was short and sweet."

"Sure was," replied Joe. "It was extra-fast because the

prosecutor's office didn't object. We all knew we didn't have anywhere near enough evidence to even contemplate bringing LaCroix to trial."

"True. But it was effective in getting LaCroix to admit he lied about his alibi."

"Definitely. Now what?"

"Joe, how about we show that restaurant waitress photos of LaCroix and Lovett and see if she identifies one of them as Knox's secret dinner companion?"

"Good idea. Let's call and find out what time she starts work today."

Back at the station, Joe called the restaurant and learned that Rosa was scheduled to start at four o'clock.

Just then Detective Caruso said that there were a Mr. and Mrs. Knox downstairs to see Ginny. Ginny went down and brought them upstairs. She and Joe sat with them in the conference room. After introductions and sympathies were expressed, Mr. Knox said, "We called dear Rick yesterday when we arrived, but couldn't reach him. We thought he could help us get into Katie's house."

"What a darling boy," said Mrs. Knox. "We were so surprised and disappointed when he and Katie got divorced. They were so in love, and he was so good to her."

"Hold on, Dear. Let me finish. Do either of you happen to know where Rick is? I know they're divorced, but I was surprised he wasn't at the funeral. Maybe he's out of town on business. Do you know?"

"Mr. and Mrs. Knox, it wasn't his fault that he wasn't available yesterday afternoon or this morning."

"Oh, where was he? And do you know where he is now?" asked Mr. Knox.

"Yes, in fact we do," said Joe. "He's available now, but from yesterday afternoon until a short while ago, he was in jail."

"In jail. My God. For what? It must have been some mistake."

"For suspicion in the death of your daughter."

"What? That can't be. Not Rick."

"I'm afraid it is. But, he was released late this morning."

"So that means he's no longer a suspect."

"No, 'fraid it doesn't," said Ginny. "Just means he's free for now, waiting to see whether or not a trial is to follow."

"How can this be?" asked Mrs. Knox. "They were so in love. Rick would have done anything for Katie."

"Mr. and Mrs. Knox, how close have you been with your daughter these past few years? How knowledgeable were you with the details of their marriage? And their divorce?"

"As much as any loving parents," said Mrs. Knox, "although with us living so far apart, we couldn't be too involved. And Katie, of course, was always very private about her personal life."

"Our understanding is that their marriage wasn't as smooth as it may have seemed. At least the few years before the divorce. And apparently, the divorce was something less than a friendly affair. But now that Mr. LaCroix has been released, you can check things out directly with him."

"We definitely will."

Ginny and Joe then spent a few minutes learning more about Knox's earlier years at home, but heard nothing useful for the case. It seemed very unlikely that the murderer was someone from her long-ago past in Massa-chusetts. Ginny then escorted the Knoxes to the medical examiner's area, where they were able to view their daughter's body and review with the assistant medical examiner the logistics and timing of getting her body back to Massachusetts.

The Knoxes left to find LaCroix, and then to go by Katie's house. Ginny returned to the station house.

Joe and Ginny were more than ready for lunch at Sancho's. They invited the other detectives in the room to join them, and Jones and Klein accepted. Caruso declined, claiming he had an important appointment over lunch. After much prodding and joking by the others, he confessed that his important appointment was for a haircut.

The four detectives had an enjoyable lunch, and were back at work within an hour. Most of the lunch discussion focused on the Knoxes, what they must be going through and all the shocks and surprises that had hit them over the past few days.

Later that afternoon, Joe and Ginny headed to Lennox to see Rosa.

Walking into La Pentola, they immediately spotted Rosa arranging place settings at a large table in the left front corner. Walking over, Ginny said, "Hi, Rosa. Remember us?"

"Sure. You're the two detectives from Jasper Creek."

"Yes," said Joe. "We'd like to show you a couple of photos to see if one of them is the man that accompanied Ms. Knox here for dinner all the time."

"Sure. Anything I can do to help you find her killer. What a shame."

Looking first at a photo of LaCroix, Rosa shook her head from side to side and said, "No, that's not him. His face was a lot thinner than the man in the photo. Plus, his hair had more gray in it. It was straighter and longer, and combed straight back. The guy in the photo almost has a crew cut."

"OK. Your comments are helpful," said Ginny. "How about this one?" she asked as she showed Lovett's photo to Rosa.

Rosa took a minute or two to carefully examine the photo. Then she said, "No, I don't think that's him either. But this one is closer. The man in the photo has a very short and thick neck. The man who ate here had a much longer and thinner neck. You could almost describe it as elegant. He also had a straighter and thinner nose than the guy in this photo."

"Sounds like you were more sure of your 'no' to the first photo than to the second one. Am I correct?"

"Yeah. The first one clearly wasn't the guy. I had to study the second one longer, 'cause he looked kinda similar. But I'm pretty sure it's not him either."

"OK, then," said Ginny. "Thank you for your help. We may be back again with more photos as we develop more suspects."

"Sure. No problem. Happy to try to help."

Joe and Ginny said their good-byes and drove to a nearby Lebanese restaurant for a change of pace.

"Well, Ginny, that didn't get us our killer, but Rosa's

comments are helpful in giving us a better picture of what the suspect looks like."

"Definitely. Despite the fact that she said no to our two prime suspects. We lucked out that their regular waitress is so organized and observant."

"I'll take all the help I can get. Wherever it comes from. But it sure would have been better if she clearly identified one of the two as Knox's lover boy."

"Amen to that. Now let's check out the menu and figure out what to order."

"This may be another time where I'll take all the help I can get, but from a waiter or waitress rather than a witness. This Lebanese menu is all Greek to me," said Joe with a smile.

CHAPTER 12

Monday morning, Ginny received a phone call. "Good morning, Detective. This is Sergeant Callahan of the Lennox PD."

"Good morning, Sergeant. What can I do for you?"

"Actually, I think I can do something for you."

"Oh?"

"Yes. We got a call yesterday afternoon from a woman who lives here in Lennox. Claims she recognized that finance lady, Knox, that was killed in your neck of the woods a week or so ago."

"Nice of her to call. But we already have a solid ID of the vic. Found her wallet with photo IDs, plus several people recognized her."

"No. This woman recognized her as the tenant in an apartment near hers. Never knew her name until she saw the news about her funeral, but surely recognized her as her neighbor."

"Oh, sorry. I misunderstood what you were saying. That's different. We'd like to swing by ASAP and talk with her. Can you arrange that? And join us? Also, can you please seal off the apartment until we can get our technicians there?"

"Yes to all of that. She's a stay-at-home mom with a young child, so we can visit her whenever you make it here. And we've already sealed the apartment."

"Good for you. You're way ahead of us. How about ten o'clock?"

"Works for me."

"Super. Where can we meet you?"

"Probably simplest to meet up at the station. Then you can follow me over to the apartment."

"Great. We'll get to your place a little before ten. And thanks for all your help."

"Don't mention it. See you shortly."

Ginny filled Joe in. At 9:30, they were in Joe's car on their way to Lennox.

They met Sergeant Callahan at the Lennox Police Department and followed him to the garden apartment complex at 1311 Jewell Street. They parked both cars in the street in front of Building C, followed the walkway to near the center of the building and knocked on the door to unit C-205.

"Coming. One second."

The door opened and there stood an attractive, but disheveled, red-haired woman who looked to be in her late 20s or early 30s.

"Hello again, Sergeant."

"Hello, Mrs. Rask." Pointing to each of the two detectives, he continued, "These are Detectives Harris and McFarland, from Jasper Creek."

Greetings were exchanged, and Rask led them into the apartment. The small foyer led to a staircase. They all followed Rask up the staircase into a small but pleasantly furnished living room, with a playpen holding what looked to be a one-year-old boy in one corner of the room.

"Thank you for meeting with us, Mrs. Rask," said Ginny.

"Oh, you're very welcome. And, please, call me Lynne. I still can't believe it."

"Mrs. Ra . . . er, Lynne, please walk us through it."

"Sure. Like I said when I called the police department, and then this morning when the sergeant here came by, I was home alone. I mean, alone except for my young son. My husband is on a ten-day business trip in Oregon and Washington, and the west coast of Canada."

"And then what happened?"

"I was watching one of the local news shows, and they talked about the death and funeral of that Knox lady. I couldn't believe it when they showed her photo. She's the lady that rents one of the apartments here."

"How well did you know her?" asked Joe.

"Not at all. She and her husband must travel a lot. They're rarely here, and they come and go at odd hours, mostly at night."

"What name did she use? And what name did her husband use?"

"No idea. We never really spoke. Or introduced ourselves. We'd wave or nod when we saw each other, but that's about it."

Showing Rask a picture of Knox, Ginny asked, "Is this her?"

"Yes, definitely."

Then, showing her a photo of LaCroix, Ginny asked if that was the husband.

"No. Same general type, but that's not him."

Ginny got the same response when she showed Rask a photo of Lovett.

"Can you describe the husband?" asked Ginny.

"Not too well. He was mostly what I'd call regular. Probably a little under six feet, mostly dark hair. Not fat or thin. Good looking. I mean, not super handsome, but not ugly by any means."

"Any distinguishing scars or tattoos? Did you ever hear him speak? Did he have an accent?"

"No to all that. He did dress well. Had an expensive-looking overcoat. That's about it."

"That's helpful," said Ginny. "How long have they rented the apartment?"

"Hard to say exactly. But I'd guess about five or six months."

"How often were they there?"

"That's a tough one. I mean, I don't hover at the window looking out at the parking lot. I probably saw them coming or going once a week or so, but I'd guess they also came and went when I didn't see them. It's not like these apartments are off a hallway or something like that. And we don't share a common garage. As you saw, each apartment's door opens right to the outside. Inside the door, there's a staircase — the one we just walked up, and a door to the two-car garage. Each apartment has its rooms on the second floor, above the garage belonging to that apartment."

"We understand. Were Ms. Knox and the man you identified as her husband always together?"

"Usually, but not always. Sometimes I just saw her or him. Are you saying that the man wasn't her husband?"

"No. We're not saying or implying anything. Just trying

to be as accurate as possible, without assuming anything," said Joe.

"Oh, I see."

"Did you see the cars that she or he or they used?"

"Yeah, a couple of times. A fairly large car, either dark blue or black. Never got a really good look. Many times, they'd drive into their garage and shut the door."

"Understood. Anything else you can tell us?" asked Ginny.

"No, I don't think so."

"When do you expect your husband to be back?"

"Thursday evening."

"OK, Mrs., er, Lynne, we'll probably be back to ask your husband the same things we've asked you. Also, as we generate more suspects, we may be back to show more photos to both of you. We may also ask you and your husband to sit with our sketch artist."

"That would be fine."

Joe and Ginny gave Rask their cards and said good-bye. Then, the two detectives and the sergeant left.

They stopped at the apartment of the complex's superintendent. It was on the end of Building B and had a large, identifying sign in front of it. The superintendent couldn't add to what Rask had told them. Asked about the name on the lease, after checking his list of apartment numbers and tenants' names, he indicated that it was leased by a firm called Fourth Institute. But he told the detectives that other than that, everything, including the rent payments, was handled in the landlord's corporate office in Columbus. He gave Ginny the name of a contact at corporate that she could call, as well as a phone number. On the way out, the detectives checked the mailroom, but the box for that apartment had no name on it.

The sergeant then led Joe and Ginny to apartment C-217, which was a half-dozen doors down from Rask's apartment. The door was cordoned off with crime scene tape, and a Lennox police officer was sitting outside the door on what looked to be a kitchen chair. He jumped up and stood at attention as soon as he saw the sergeant leading Joe and Ginny his way.

While the sergeant stayed outside, Joe and Ginny put on disposable gloves and entered the apartment. The foyer, staircase and door to the garage were identical to those in Rask's apartment. Because there were muddy footprints on the foyer floor and the staircase, Joe and Ginny decided not to proceed through the apartment. There were also what appeared to be dried blood stains on the floor. To ensure that they wouldn't mess up or destroy any evidence, they decided to wait until the Crime Scene team worked its way through the apartment. They did open the door to the garage and peek in. Not surprisingly, there were no cars in the garage.

Joe and Ginny, with the sergeant as their local escort, tried to talk with as many neighbors as they could. They knocked on close to 20 doors, and got to speak with someone at about half the apartments they tried. Most of the people they spoke with knew nothing about Knox's death or funeral. When showed her photo, most recognized her as living in the complex but had little additional information. A few had seen her with a man, but were unable to confirm whether either of the photos Ginny showed them was the man they had seen with Knox.

Joe, Ginny and the sergeant returned to their cars. Thanks and good-byes, and Joe and Ginny were on their way back to Jasper Creek. En route, Ginny called the Crime Scene supervisor and told him his technicians needed to carefully check the apartment in Lennox. She gave the supervisor a summary of the background so he'd know exactly what to look for. She also gave him Sergeant Callahan's name and contact information so that they could coordinate their work with him.

After a quick lunch at Sancho's around the corner from the station, Joe and Ginny spent most of the afternoon trying to track down who had leased the apartment in Lennox. Turned out that the lessee was a private corporation. Then, checking with the Ohio Secretary of State's office, Joe was led to one legal entity owned another, which in turn was owned by a third. For each entity, Joe obtained the recorded agent, owners and officers, after which he searched for the backgrounds of all these individuals. By the time he was finished he had a string of corporations, all of which listed fictitious agents, owners, directors and officers.

At the same time, Ginny was following the trail of how the monthly rent was paid. Turns out it was paid each month by a money order mailed to the landlord. No return address on the envelopes, and no identification on the money orders. The source of the money orders varied — the post office, Walmart, several supermarkets and drug chains, and so on. Tracking the lessee, or lessees, would not be an easy task.

Around 4:30, Ginny received a call from the Crime Scene supervisor.

"Hi, Detective. This is Bob Branson. We're back from that apartment in Lennox."

"Hi, Bob. And?"

"And we got a whole lot of stuff for Forensics to process."

"Anything that might be interesting?"

"We'll know more in a day or two, but I think so. First off, as you might expect, there are a million fingerprints. Can't tell how long they've been there, but Forensics'll run 'em all through the various databases. More interestingly, some small amounts of blood at the bottom of the interior staircase. Don't know yet if it's the vic's. Hell, we don't even know yet if it's human. But we'll be finding out. It does appear that someone stepped in the blood. Not enough to get a shoe print, but there's a shoe out there someplace with traces of this blood on it. We also took photographs and molds of the muddy footprints in that foyer, and on the steps and upstairs. Can't use these to identify someone up front like fingerprints often can, but they can confirm or disqualify possible suspects once you have some. You'll need the ME to confirm whether the COD was the vic's fall or something else, but, cause of death or not, she clearly fell, by accident or with some help, down the flight of stairs between the front-door foyer and the living room. And, perhaps most interesting of all, the bedroom has two twin beds in it."

"And?"

"One bed had a bedspread on it and the other one didn't. And the bedspread looks identical to the one the vic was wrapped in in that car trunk. This apartment's very likely the crime scene."

"Wow. You guys might have hit the jackpot. Good going. Please keep us informed."

"For sure."

Hanging up, Ginny brought Joe up to speed.

"That's super. This might be the break we've been waiting for."

"Yup. But when you describe it to the chief, be sure to say that we've been working toward it, not just sitting and waiting for it."

"Natch. In fact, let's both go give him the good news now."

Joe and Ginny filled the chief in and were pleasantly surprised when he said little more than "well done." Joe viewed that as about as good as a meeting with the chief could ever go. *Except, of course, for that one meeting when he said Ginny and I could continue as partners despite our relationship. Nothing will ever top that meeting.*

When Joe and Ginny returned to their desks, there was a message to return a call from Forensics.

"Hello. Sorensen in Forensics. How may I help you?"

"Hi, Christen. Ginny Harris. Sorry I missed your call earlier."

"Not a problem. I'm sure you were busy chasing down bad guys. We finished a bunch of our analyses. Figured I'd give you a verbal rather than making you wait for the written report."

"Appreciate that." Ginny put the call on speaker, and Joe and Sorensen said hello to each other.

"First off, nothing unusual in Mr. LaCroix's garage or

car. Of course, a large number of unidentified prints, but nothing suspicious looking. With all the snow falling and wind blowing, there were no footprints in the driveway snow."

"Too bad. Not surprised," said Joe. "But we appreciate the report. Anything else?"

"A lot of prints from the victim's house and car. Other than the victim's prints, the rest are unidentified. And there was nothing else useful in the vic's car, or any of the stuff that was picked up in that parking lot in Lennox where her car was found. That's it so far."

"OK, Christen. Thanks," said Ginny.

To celebrate the crime scene almost surely having been identified, Joe and Ginny had dinner at an upscale Indian restaurant not far from Joe's house.

CHAPTER 13

First thing the next morning, Joe and Ginny returned to the apartment in Lennox. Ginny had called Sergeant Callahan. Since the apartment was empty, he didn't feel the need to accompany them. He did, however, radio the uniformed officer at the apartment so that Joe and Ginny would have no trouble entering it.

Joe and Ginny spent less than an hour there. They were able to conduct a thorough investigation, as there was very little to examine. There was a bare minimum of inexpensive but functional furniture. Not much else, other than the blood stains and muddy footprints they already knew about.

"Jeez, Joe, there's even less food here in the fridge and cabinets than at your house."

"Yeah, and the garage is just as empty. A broom, a trash can and extra garbage bags. That's about it."

"And only the bare minimum of clothing, like one or two outfits and sets of underwear."

"And, Ginny, you'd never survive with the teensy amount of makeup in the bathroom. You'd refuse to be seen in public."

"Very funny. But no one was actually living here. It's more like their secret hideaway for a little you-know-what."

"Yes, I do know what. And I think you're right. It sure

would be helpful if we could find out who the other half of the duo was."

"Sure would. Let's hope Forensics can identify a fingerprint. Or DNA from the toothbrush, or a hair that was in the bathroom."

"I'm hoping with all my strength."

"Oh, you're such a great hoper, Joe."

"Well, golly gee, that's the nicest thing you've said to me today," said Joe with a big grin.

"Just wait. It's still early. It might get even better."

Joe and Ginny left the apartment and returned to Jasper Creek.

Back at their desks, Ginny said, "Joe, let's take a couple of minutes and summarize where we are on this case. All subject, of course, to what we'll learn from Forensics, hopefully this afternoon or tomorrow."

"OK, I'll start. Despite various versions of 'no' from Rosa over at La Pentola and Mrs. Rask over in Lennox, LaCroix and Lovett are still our two best bets."

"Agreed. But although not as likely, LaCroix's girlfriend, that Ray woman, is still a possibility. Maybe she found out, or at least imagined, that LaCroix and Knox were secretly back at it again."

"Could be. And she could have opened the trunk at the supermarket just to prove she couldn't be the killer, 'cause the murderer wouldn't be dumb enough to open it in public."

"We've seen things way wilder than that, Joe."

"Of course, we also have a whole field of other possible suspects, with unknown motives, who could've chosen LaCroix's car as a handy hiding place for the body. The real lover of Knox, that lover's wife or girlfriend, some enemy she made at work, or who knows what."

"True. But that's the situation in almost every case. For now, let's stick with the suspects we know."

"Fair enough. In fact, I'm going to the body shop to drag Lovett back here again. We need to press him as hard as we pressed LaCroix. Maybe some worthwhile juice will squeeze out."

"Go for it. I'll be here when you and he get back."

Joe hopped into his car and was soon at Sunshine Auto. He walked in and spoke with Delmond, the manager.

"Good morning, Detective. Back again? We'll have to give you a reserved parking space pretty soon. How can I help you this morning?"

"Good morning. I'd like to speak with Bill Lovett again."

"Me too."

"Huh? What does that mean?"

"After you spoke with him last week, he finished his day's work, and that was it. Didn't show again. I called more than a few times. Left voicemails, but he hasn't called me back."

"Any idea why? Or where he might be?"

"Nope. Maybe he got hit by a car or something. Or maybe you scared the hell out of him. Or, who knows? A damn shame, he was a good worker. And very dependable — until now."

"Mr. Delmond, I'd like to take a look at his employment application. It might say who his emergency contact is. Also, I'll want to check with his prior employers."

"Sure. Hold on a sec." Desmond spun around in his chair, opened a file drawer in the credenza behind him and pulled out a file. "Here it is. Just a couple of pages. Let me make a copy for you."

Desmond walked across his small office to the photocopier in the corner, copied the three pages in Lovett's file and gave the copies to Joe.

"Thank you. Please give me a call if you hear from him, or learn anything about his whereabouts."

"Sure will. And I very well might. We still have his paycheck for the part of last week that he worked."

Joe said good-bye and returned to the station.

"Ginny, our warm suspect just got hotter."

"Oh. I gather something's up. Where's Lovett? Hope you didn't forget and leave him in your car."

"Very funny. No. He's AWOL. It was Wednesday when we talked with him, right? He never showed up for work after Wednesday, and no call to the body shop."

"Sounds suspicious, given our disbelief in coincidence."

"Yup. I have a copy of his personnel file. We'll see if there's anything useful in it."

Joe and Ginny quickly scanned through the three pages. It showed the same local address that Lovett had provided earlier, the names of two people he had given as references when applying for work at Sunshine Auto, and his prior two employers, a body shop in Oshkosh, Wisconsin, followed by a muffler manufacturer in Columbus, Ohio. A separate handwritten sheet described Lovett's conviction for attempted rape and murder in one of the suburbs of Milwaukee and his seven years in prison in Waupun, Wisconsin.

"Ginny, let's head over to his apartment now and see what we can discover."

"Let's go, I'm ready," said Ginny as she stood up and started toward the door.

Twenty minutes later, Joe was knocking on the door of apartment 346 at 1213 March Street. When there was no answer, Joe and Ginny went back to the first floor and located the building super's apartment.

"Yes? Can I help you?" asked the thin, elderly super as he opened his door in response to Ginny's knock.

"Yes. I'm Detective Harris, and this is Detective McFarland," said Ginny as she and Joe flashed their badges. "We're trying to locate one of your tenants, Bill Lovett in apartment 346. We knocked but no one answered."

"Not home, I guess."

"Do you know him?" asked Joe.

"Recognize the name, but not sure if I'd recognize him. We have a lot of tenants, and they're often moving out and moving in." After checking the sheet of paper he kept on the table near the door, the super said, "Pays his rent on time every month. In fact, he's paid up 'til the end of this month."

"We'd like to see his apartment. Can you let us in?" asked Ginny.

"Well, I'm not sure I'm supposed to. Don't you need a warrant or something?"

"We can get one and return. But we fear something may have happened to Mr. Lovett, and we shouldn't waste any time."

"Oh, that's different. Let me grab my master key and we'll head on up."

Joe and Ginny were soon in Lovett's apartment, with the super on his way back downstairs.

Joe and Ginny thoroughly searched the apartment in less than 30 minutes. There was a bare minimum of furniture: a couch with a side table, and a TV on another side table in the living room; a folding bridge table with two folding chairs in the kitchen; and a bed, night table and three-drawer dresser in the bedroom. A few lamps, and that was it. All the furniture looked like it had been purchased used, well past its prime. Two stacks of papers on the kitchen table and a bunch of papers in one of the dresser drawers were it in terms of documents. Various work pants and shirts, a few sets of non-work casual clothes, and a drawer with a few pieces of underwear and three pairs of socks, plus one of each of the essential toiletry items in the bathroom, rounded out his belongings.

"He clearly moved in here with a minimum of expense and effort, and probably hasn't added much since day one. I wonder if he's moved elsewhere or is planning on coming back. Hard to tell based on the few pieces of clothing here."

"You're right. Jeez, Joe, I probably do more to personalize a hotel room that I spend one night in," said Ginny.

"Well, it sure wouldn't take much to do more than Lovett did here. There's nothing that tells us anything."

"That's for sure. Even his papers are the bare minimum. Receipts for his rent and cell phone payments, the last few days' newspapers, title for his car, and that's it."

"I bet he's thinking as if he's still in prison. This apartment is just another cell he moved into. And you don't get to do too much personalizing of your prison cell."

"Could be. But that was quite a few years ago."

"Well, that's for the shrinks. Let's schedule a visit to the muffler plant he worked at in Columbus before he started working at Sunshine Auto."

"OK. Want me to call them?"

"That's OK. I got it."

Joe got the number of Majestic Muffler from information and called the company. After being transferred a couple of times, he spoke with Lovett's former foreman and scheduled a visit for three that afternoon.

Joe and Ginny left the apartment, stopped at the super's and reminded him to lock Lovett's door. Joe gave him his card and asked to be called if the super thought of anything, or especially if he saw Lovett.

Joe and Ginny returned to the station. They joined two of the other detectives for lunch at a nearby pizza parlor. After lunch, the two other detectives returned to the station while Joe and Ginny got into Joe's car and headed for Columbus.

Joe and Ginny arrived at Majestic Muffler almost a half-hour early, but Lovett's former foreman was available and happy to meet early.

Sitting in the small lunch room, each with a cup of coffee, Joe started right in. "Mr. Ingersoll, thanks for meeting with us on such short notice."

"Not a problem. What can I do for you? All you said on the phone was that you wanted to talk about Bill Lovett."

"Yes, that's correct," said Ginny. "We're having trouble locating him. He's not at his work or apartment. We thought you might know something that can help."

"Hate to say it, but I think you made a wasted trip here. Bill worked here for about 18 months, and then quit to go to work for an auto body shop about eight or nine months ago. I haven't seen or spoken with him since he left."

"How about some of his co-workers?" asked Joe. "Anyone he was close to that he might have stayed in touch with?"

"Nope. He was a decent worker. Not great, but he did what he was supposed to do without me having to be all over him. But he was super quiet. Or maybe private's a better word. Other than things like the weather and the prior night's baseball scores, he barely spoke to anyone here, including me."

"Oh. Did he seem to be hiding something?" asked Ginny.

"Don't think so, but you can never be sure. I think it was more a habit he learned while he was in prison."

"Oh, so you knew about that?"

"Definitely. He was upfront about it when he applied. And our owner has a soft spot for ex-cons who've paid for their crime, so to say. He gives quite a few of them jobs here."

"And how's that work out?" asked Joe.

"Usually pretty good. Once in a while you get a bad apple. But, hell, you get bad apples in groups of non-ex-cons also."

"Did everyone know about his prison stint?" asked Ginny.

"Nope. Just the owner, our office manager and me, as his foreman. He was free to tell others if he wished, but he didn't. And we keep stuff like that confidential."

"Mr. Ingersoll, did he have any problems with anger management stuff while he was here?" asked Ginny.

"No. None. In fact, either he never got upset about anything, or he hid it real well."

"Any idea where he might be now? Where we might look for him?"

"No. Sorry. I didn't know that much about him when he worked here, and I surely don't know any more about him now."

"OK. Well, thank you for your time, Mr. Ingersoll. Here's my card. Please call if you think of anything, or if you hear from him."

"Sure will."

Joe and Ginny were soon back in Joe's car. They stopped at a supermarket in Jasper Creek, had dinner at Joe's house and were asleep by ten.

CHAPTER 14

The next morning, Ginny called Lovett's previous employer in Oshkosh while Joe spoke with the detective who handled Lovett's attempted rape and murder case. Neither had anything of value to add. Joe then used his speaker phone to call the prison in Wisconsin where Lovett served his seven years. It took quite a while to be put in touch with the assistant warden, who had been a corrections officer supervisor during Lovett's time and had served in Lovett's cell block. Here also, to the degree that the assistant warden could remember, Lovett had been a loner and hadn't, as many inmates do, made any friends or joined a gang.

"Boy, Lovett sure doesn't leave much of a trail," said Ginny.

"That's for sure. But, despite that, he's still one of our star suspects. Now all we have to do is find him."

"Correct. And how do you propose we do that?"

"Hang on, Ginny. I'm thinking."

"I'm hanging on real tight. I can already hear those rusty gears in your head starting to turn."

"Hey, they're not rusty. They've just been sitting quietly and patiently until we needed them to start turning."

"Ah, OK. Turn away."

"All set. Here's my master plan. Other than issuing BOLOs between here and Wisconsin on both Lovett and his car, we put him aside for now."

"That's it?"

"No. There's more. While we're waiting for Forensics to get back to us with what they learned from the evidence found in the Lennox apartment, I say we squeeze LaCroix's girlfriend."

"Doesn't sound like much of a plan. But it's more than I can come up with. So let's run with it."

"OK. Why don't you do your computer magic and get those BOLOs issued? Just to show you what a great partner I am, while you're doing that I'll bring the chief up to speed. And then, I'll head out and bring back some lunch for us. After that we'll head out to National Pipe and pop in on Ray."

"Deal."

Joe walked down the hall and spent about ten minutes with the chief. Joe filled him in on what they'd been doing, their current plans with the BOLOs and the Ray interrogation. Like Joe, the chief was hopeful that Forensics would uncover something useful from everything that had been gathered up in the apartment in Lennox. Joe was surprised and relieved at how non-aggressive and non-antagonistic the chief was. *He must have taken his meds this morning.*

Walking back toward his desk, Joe loudly announced that he was going to bring back Chinese food for himself and Ginny and would be happy to bring back whatever anyone else might want. Ten minutes later, Joe had lunch orders and money from seven others in the room. Realizing Joe'd never be able to carry everything back to the station, especially with four soup orders, Detective Jones went with him to help carry the food.

Joe and Jones made it back about 40 minutes later. Nothing had spilled or been dropped. Everyone thanked them and stopped working to eat together at the same time. There was even a good bit of socializing and teasing of each other. This was a rare occasion in the department, and Joe was pleased that he had initiated it by offering to pick up lunches. The chief would surely recognize how he and Ginny were increasing their social interactions with others in the department.

Having finished their soups, wonton for Joe and hot and sour for Ginny, and lo mein, Joe and Ginny got into Ginny's car and took off for National Pipe.

A half-hour later, Joe and Ginny were sitting opposite Ray at a square table in an empty office on the second floor of National Pipe.

"What is it now, Detectives? I've already told you everything I know."

"Have you really?" asked Joe.

"What? Yes, I have. What are you saying?"

"We think you haven't told us everything yet," said Ginny.

Leaning forward with her hands balled into fists, Ray said, "What are you talking about? Like what?"

"Like your boyfriend and Ms. Knox."

"I already told you. How they were married for a long time, and then they got divorced. Then Rick stopped working here."

"Yes, you did. But we meant more recently."

"Huh? What are you talking about?"

"We want to know how you found out that the two of them started seeing each other again."

"What? You're mistaken. They haven't. Hell, Rick couldn't stand her."

"Rather perfect cover for a little hanky-panky. Wouldn't you say?" asked Joe.

"You're wrong. Dead wrong. Rick and I are in love. We're even planning our wedding."

"Yup. Best to fool around some while you're still single."

Ray slapped her hand flat, loudly, on the tabletop and jumped to her feet. "That's it, we're done. If you have some proof let me know, otherwise I'm out of here. Now."

"You're free to go," said Ginny. "For now. Just don't leave town without contacting one of us first."

"Am I a suspect now? What's wrong with you two?"

"For now, let's say 'person of interest' rather than 'suspect.' But that can change."

"This is ridiculous. I'm leaving now."

"Fine. Have a nice day. We'll be in touch, I'm sure," said Joe.

Ray stormed out of the door and down the stairs in record time. Joe and Ginny returned to Ginny's car.

"Wow. That's one pissed-off lady," said Ginny. "We sure did a number on her."

"Yes, we did. But her surprise and anger seemed genuine. Either she's a much better actress than we thought, or there's nothing there. Even if they were seeing each other, I'm pretty sure Ray didn't know about it."

"Full agreement. But I'd love to hear what she says to LaCroix, and what his reaction is."

"Ditto."

"OK. Now the big question, Joe. Where to? It's too early to go home or have dinner. But it's too late to get much done at the station."

"How about we head back and pop in on Forensics? They ought to have something by now."

"Good idea. And by the time we're done there, it'll almost be a respectable time for dinner. How about Pithari's tonight? I have a sudden urge for Greek."

"Sudden food urge. You're not pregnant, are you?"

"No. Don't worry, Joe. I'll let you know when."

"Whew. What a relief."

Ginny parked in the PD parking lot and she and Joe walked into the Forensics lab. Ginny couldn't help noticing that, like whenever she visited, the lab was deadly quiet. There were only a few employees working at tables, but there were bags and envelopes of crime scene "stuff" sitting and stacked everywhere. She was always amazed that they didn't seem to ever lose or mix up evidence between cases.

Joe and Ginny walked up to Sorensen, the Forensics supervisor.

"Hi, Christen," said Ginny as Joe nodded.

"Hi, Detectives. What can I do for you?'

"Not pushing you, Christen. Well, actually we are a bit. Anxious to know what you have so far from that apartment in Lennox."

"Why aren't I surprised? In fact, we're close to wrapping it up. Let's go into my office, or more precisely my cramped cubicle, and I can bring you up to speed."

Joe and Ginny followed Sorensen through a pair of swinging doors into a rectangular room with six cubicles in it. Stepping into his small cubicle, Sorensen sat in the chair behind his desk. Joe and Ginny sat in the two undersized chairs in front of the desk.

"OK, let me grab the right file," said Sorensen as he sorted through about ten files scattered all over his desk. "Here it is. Knox," he said, holding one file over his head like it was a championship hockey trophy.

Opening the file, Sorensen began summarizing select facts from the draft report. "Many different sets of prints. Still running them to try to get some identifications. Knox, the vic, was clearly one of them. No idea, of course, how long some of these prints have been there. Could be a couple of days. Or a couple of years. The blood at the bottom of the stairs is clearly the vic's. Also confirmed that the bedspread in the apartment is the twin of the spread the vic was wrapped in."

"That's some useful info," said Ginny. "Anything else?"

"Crime Scene confirmed no forced entry, so whoever else was there either had a key or was let in by the vic. The door automatically locks when it closes, and it was locked when the police first got there."

"When do you expect to be finished running the prints?" asked Joe.

"Probably sometime tomorrow afternoon."

"Any usable DNA samples from the stuff in the bathroom? Or kitchen?"

"Yes, but I'm going to try to keep it a secret from you two for as long as possible . . . . Just kidding. The DNA will take another couple of days. Not to worry, I'll call you as soon as we're done. Oh, and one other thing."

"What's that?"

"The car the vic was found in had prints from the owner and his girlfriend, Ray, plus a bunch of others we can't identify. No other scraps of anything. We and your IT department both went through the cell phone that was in the vic's pocketbook. A bunch of what look to be work-related phone calls and texts, plus a call almost every week to her parents' home in Massachusetts. And the normal bunch of calls to restaurants, stores, contractors and so on. I'll send the list over to you, but I doubt it merits much of your time."

"Thanks, Christen," said Ginny. "Appreciate all your help."

"That's what we're here for. Have a good one."

"Same to you," said Joe.

Joe and Ginny headed to Pithari's.

Back at Joe's house after an enjoyable dinner, the heavy meal and wine had them both fast asleep by nine.

CHAPTER 15

Between bites of her toasted bagel the next morning, Ginny said, "I can't wait to hear what Forensics found with all those fingerprints and the DNA samples."

"Me, too. Hope it points us right to the perp."

"Would be nice to have an easy one like that for a change."

"Sure would, Ginny. But given our luck, let's not count on it."

"For sure."

Back at their desks, Joe's phone rang around 9:15.

"Hello. Detective McFarland. How can I help you?"

"What the hell do you think you're doing?"

"Excuse me. Who's this?"

"This is Rick LaCroix. Susie told me what you and your partner accused her of yesterday. Are you nuts? How can you even think she might have anything to do with Kathryn's death? And where'd you get the cockeyed idea that Kathryn and I were seeing each other? Hell, she couldn't stand me any more than I could put up with her."

"Calm down, Mr. LaCroix. We're just doing our job. Like it or not, Ms. Ray and, even more so, you are suspects."

"Is that the best you can come up with?"

"Yes, it is. For the moment. We're looking at other scenarios as well, but so far you're up near the top of our list."

"That's crazy."

"Maybe. But it's a fact that, of all the cars in the world, the body ended up in your trunk. Not to mention you and Ms. Knox had a relationship, and a rocky one at that, when your marriage ended. And, not only don't you have a solid alibi for the time of death, you lied to us about where you were and what time you got home from work that evening."

"I already explained to you that I lied because I knew it would look bad if I told you the truth."

"Well, you were right about that. It does look bad."

"Fine. Think whatever you want. But you ought to be working to find out who the killer is, rather than wasting time on Susie and me."

"Thank you very much for your advice, but I think we're capable of managing our own investigation."

"Yeah, well, it sure doesn't seem that way."

And before Joe could reply, LaCroix had angrily hung up.

Joe filled Ginny in on LaCroix's side of the conversation.

"If nothing else, we definitely got his attention."

"Yup. And if he's upset enough, maybe he'll do something stupid. Let's hope so."

Joe and Ginny spent the rest of the morning catching up on paperwork. Back at their desks after lunch, Ginny's phone rang.

"Detective Harris?"

"Yes. Speaking. Who is this?"

"Sergeant Dieter with the Cleveland PD. We got a hit on your BOLO. The car's been located in a motel parking lot here in Cleveland."

"Oh, that's great. Any sign of the owner, a William Lovett?"

"No. We checked with the front desk. No Lovett registered. But most of their business is cash, so who knows which names are real? We've been watching the car, but no action so far."

"Super. We'll head to Cleveland right now. It'll probably take three-and-a-half, four hours."

"Not a problem. We'll be here. Why don't you call me when you're about 30 minutes out and I'll meet you at the motel? It's the Cascade Inn at 3224 East 24th Street, right downtown."

"OK. Appreciate your help. We'll call you in a few hours as we get close."

"Sounds like a plan. See you later."

Ginny hung up and filled Joe in. Ten minutes later, they were in Joe's car, heading for Cleveland.

As planned, Ginny called Dieter when their GPS said they had about 30 minutes to go. Dieter met them around the corner from the motel 40 minutes later. After introductions, Dieter spoke with the plainclothes cop watching the car. Still no activity.

About 5:30, the plainclothes detective radioed Dieter to say that a man had entered the car and was getting ready to drive away. Dieter told him to intercept the driver, and that he and the two Jasper Creek detectives would be there in less than a minute.

Two minutes later, Joe and Ginny, accompanied by Dieter, were face-to-face with a surprised and worried-looking Lovett.

"What a surprise," said Joe. "Small world, meeting you here."

"What's going on? Why are you stopping me?"

"Why'd you run and hide?" asked Ginny.

"What? I didn't. You told me to let you know if I was going to leave Ohio. Well, guess what, last I checked Cleveland is still part of Ohio."

"Yes, it is. Let's head over to Detective Dieter's station and have a more detailed discussion."

"Am I under arrest? Do I have to go with you?"

"No to both questions," answered Ginny. "But your life will probably be a whole lot better if you voluntarily come with us for a brief discussion."

"OK. But what about my car?"

"You can leave it parked here at the motel for the time being."

Twenty minutes later, Joe, Ginny, Dieter and Lovett were squeezed into a small interrogation room at Dieter's station house.

Joe made the standard introduction of who, when and where into the tape recorder, and then read Lovett his Miranda rights.

"Mr. Lovett, what are you doing here in Cleveland? And how come you left Jasper Creek without even telling your boss?"

"I'm here looking for a job."

"Oh, what's wrong with your job at Sunshine Auto?"

"Nothing. I actually liked the work. And they were real good to me."

"But?"

"You started nosing around. I've seen it before. Because

of my record, I'd never get a fair chance with you. The cops always blame the ex-con."

"You may think that, but that's not the case," said Ginny.

"Yeah. Sure. I've seen it too many times already. So I decided to leave the area and find a new job someplace else."

"Why Cleveland? You know someone here?"

"No. It was about as far as I could get from Jasper Creek without leaving the state and having to tell you where I was going."

"Mr. Lovett," said Joe, "why don't I believe you're telling us everything?"

"Like I said, that's how you view all ex-cons."

"What was your relationship with Kathryn Knox? Or did you just see her one day without even knowing who she was?" asked Joe.

"Neither. I didn't know her, had never even heard of her until after her murder."

"And why should we believe you didn't commit the murder?"

"Because you've got no reason, much less evidence, to think I did."

"Are you sure of that?" asked Ginny.

"Definitely. Unless you're making stuff up to railroad me. Sure would be faster and easier than actually having to find the killer."

"Need I remind you that allegedly being home sick and all alone is less than a watertight alibi?" asked Ginny.

"Well, I can't help it. Like it or not, that's where I was."

"Too bad there's no one who can corroborate that for you."

"Guess I'm just unlucky."

"Mr. Lovett, are we correct that you had access to Mr. LaCroix's car?"

"Who?"

"LaCroix. Rick LaCroix. The owner of the car in which Ms. Knox's body was found."

"I have no idea. I never met the guy."

"His car was in the body shop the day before the murder."

"Then I probably did have access to it. All of us pretty much had access to all the cars being worked on. But that doesn't mean anything."

"Not by itself, it doesn't," said Joe. "But adding all these little tidbits together does begin to give it all meaning."

"Enough. Are we done yet? Or do I have to ask for a lawyer?"

"No, we're done. For now. I assume the sergeant can get someone to drive you back to your motel. Be sure to keep us informed if you relocate again. In or out of Ohio. Here's another of my cards, in case you lost the other one."

"OK."

"Oh, and one more thing," said Ginny.

"Yeah. What's that?"

"You might want to call Sunshine Auto. Besides giving them the courtesy of resigning, you might want to tell them where to send your last paycheck."

"Uh. Yeah. OK."

Joe and Ginny treated Dieter to dinner at a local Italian restaurant that he suggested. After dinner, they thanked him, said their good-byes and headed back to Jasper Creek.

It was past midnight when they reached Joe's house and tumbled into bed exhausted.

CHAPTER 16

Despite the late night, Joe and Ginny were back at their desks before eight the next morning. Ginny had a phone message that Sorensen from Forensics had called late the day before. Ginny called, but learned that Sorensen wouldn't be in until about nine. Ginny left a message for him to call her.

"Joe, I've been thinking about our session with Lovett yesterday."

"Yeah. And?"

"My gut tells me he didn't do it. Can't tell you why . . . he seemed stupid but believable to me."

"I know what you mean. He does have that dumb-but-honest look to him."

"I suggest we keep him on our suspect list, but move him out of first place."

"I'm fine with that. That leaves LaCroix as Numero Uno. I'd feel better if that waitress, Rosa, wasn't so sure he wasn't Knox's dinner partner."

"Yeah. She seemed pretty sharp. Her saying 'no' sure doesn't strengthen the case against him."

"Yup. What we have to do is find out who her dinner partner was. He presumably is also the guy who spent time with her in the Lennox apartment. Hopefully, he left fingerprints or DNA that can be identified."

About a half-hour later, Ginny's phone rang.

"Hi, Detective. Sorensen here in Forensics. We got all

we're going to get from fingerprints and DNA in that apartment."

"That's great, Christen. Joe and I will be down in a couple of minutes."

"I'll be here."

Five minutes later, Joe and Ginny were back sitting in Sorensen's cubicle, this time with everyone holding a cup of hot coffee.

"So, let's hear what you've got. The suspense is killing me," said Joe.

"OK, then. Wouldn't want you to die right here. I'd be stuck doing all kinds of paperwork."

"Yeah, it would be a shame how much my death would inconvenience you," said Joe as he chuckled.

"OK, first the fingerprints. We found full, or almost full, prints from 14 different people. One of them was easy to identify. Several sets were the vic's. Running the prints through all the usual databases let us identify four others, three of whom had their prints on file back from when they were in the military."

"And who are they?" asked Ginny.

"Again, let me remind you that we have no way to tell how long ago the prints were left there. But here are the three." Handing Ginny a sheet of paper with three names and addresses, Sorensen continued, "All three are contractors. As you can see from the sheet, two are plumbers and one is a retired electrician."

"OK. Not surprising that folks like that would at some point be in an apartment. How about the other one you identified?" asked Joe.

"That's a Robert Hastings. He's currently in prison on a

burglary charge. For all we know, he might have burglar-ized the apartment at some point."

"True. And the other prints? And the DNA?"

"No IDs on any of them. But they're solid specimens, so if there's anyone you suspect, it'd be pretty easy to check their fingerprints and DNA against these samples. Oh, and the same goes for the muddy footprints. Bring me shoes, and I'll let you know if they made those prints."

"Well, that's something," said Ginny. "Now all we need are some suspects."

"Yup," said Joe. "Maybe we can start with LaCroix and his girlfriend. And our buddy, Lovett."

"True," said Ginny.

"Thanks for all your efforts on this," said Joe. "And your expediting it. Now the ball's in our court to get some more suspects so we can get you their prints and DNA. And like I said, we'll bring you samples from our three current persons of interest."

"We'll be here."

Joe and Ginny said their good-byes and returned to their desks.

"Bummer," said Joe. "Woulda been nice if he coulda just named the killer for us."

"Sure would have. But you didn't really expect that, did you?"

"No, but a guy can hope. Can't he?"

"Sure. Hope all you want. Just don't count on it hap-pening."

"Gotcha. Now what?"

"I'm out of ideas right now, Joe. Unless you have a brainstorm, I suggest we go back to the beginning and review everything we did and learned. Maybe a new 'aha' will break through."

"Now who's counting on hope? But OK. I can't think of anything better, so let's do it."

And so Joe and Ginny started with the call they got that Saturday morning telling them about a dead woman in the trunk of a car at a Kroger supermarket. While they were reviewing each step and interview since then, often relying on their notebooks for details, Ginny's phone rang.

"Hello, this is Detective Harris."

"Good morning, Detective. This is Sergeant Callahan from Lennox."

"Hi. What's up?"

"You two just seem to keep winning the lottery."

"Oh, goody. What'd we win this time?"

"Remember that lady who recognized from TV that your victim was her neighbor?"

"Yeah. Sure do. That was a nice break for us."

"Well, she did it again."

"Huh? Whadda you mean?"

"She was watching TV again. I guess not much else to do, with a small kid and her husband out of town."

"And?"

"And she recognized the guy she assumes was the vic's husband."

"Wow. Now that's a real break in the case. Who did she say he was?"

"She didn't remember his name. But he was the vic's boss where she worked. One of our local stations was running a series on the increasing murder rate in this area, in large part driven by drug addiction. Apparently, her boss spoke at some memorial service they had for your vic, and a small sliver of his speech was on TV."

"That's super. We'd like to meet with her now. Would that be possible? Can you join us?"

"Yes and yes."

"OK. We'll meet you in front of her apartment. Say, in 30 minutes."

"I'll be there."

At 11:30, Ginny pulled up and parked in front of Rask's apartment. Sergeant Callahan was already parked there. The three of them walked to Rask's front door, and were soon again sitting with her in her living room.

"Mrs. Rask, sorry to bother you again. But we understand you have some news for us."

"Oh, please. It's no bother at all. In fact, I appreciate the few minutes of adult conversation while my husband's still out of town."

"Mrs. Rask," said Joe, "why don't you tell us what you told the sergeant earlier?"

"Sure. Happy to. I was watching, or actually more like listening to rather than watching, TV, the local news on Channel 4, when they showed a special on the increasing rate of murders in this part of Ohio. They included a short clip of a memorial service held for that dead woman."

"Oh."

"Yeah. I'm not sure I caught the whole thing, but I think the service was basically just for her co-workers at her company. Not for friends or neighbors or relatives. That caught my attention. And I looked up. Her boss was giving a speech about what a wonderful person she was, and how everyone at the company would miss her so much. Then I realized it was him."

"Him?" prodded Ginny.

"Yes, him. The man that was always here with her. The one I assumed was her husband. I still don't really know if he was her husband or not."

"Mrs. Rask, let me pull up four photographs on my cell phone. These photos are not very good, as they're from the Department of Motor Vehicles. Driver's license photos are usually pretty bad. But I'd like you to look at each picture and say whether or not that's the man."

"OK. I'll try."

Ginny used her smartphone to access the DMV database to get a photo of Knox's boss, Van Hale. She also pulled up photos of three police officers she knew who had a somewhat similar appearance to Van Hale. Ginny then showed Rask the photos one at a time.

"No, that's not him. No, way too young. Wait. Hold on. I think that's him. Yes, I'm sure it is."

Sure enough, Rask had identified Van Hale as the assumed husband. A few more minutes of discussion, and Ginny was driving back to Jasper Creek, trying her best to prevent her enthusiasm and excitement from causing her to speed too much.

"Ginny, whadda you think? Should we head right to Van Hale's office and nab him? I bet a little sweating in our interrogation room might do wonders in getting him to open up."

"Boy, I'd love to. But maybe we should see if we can get warrants to search his office and home first. Also his and his wife's cars. Then, depending on how our conversation with him goes, we can do the searches right away without worrying about him hiding or destroying anything."

"You're right. I'll call and check if we can see Porter as soon as we get back to town."

Joe called Porter's office, but he was in court. His administrative assistant said that she expected court to break for lunch at any moment. She was going to grab a sandwich for Porter so that he could get a little work done while eating before he had to go back in. Joe explained why he and Ginny wanted to see him, and Porter's assistant offered to also get sandwiches for Joe and Ginny so that the three of them could meet for a few minutes in Porter's office. Joe thanked her and said they'd be there in about ten minutes.

Joe filled Ginny in. Ginny parked in front of the courthouse, and they were in the county prosecutor's office five minutes later. Porter walked in about ten minutes later, having been briefed by his assistant.

"Hi, Ginny. Joe. Boy, you guys'll do anything for a free lunch."

"We confess. Now you know our secret," said Joe. "Seriously, this shouldn't take long. We know you need to get some work done before you're called back into court."

"Not a problem. Whadda ya have?"

Joe and Ginny, often interrupting each other, gave Porter a brief summary of the case, where they were on it, the neighbor's identification of Van Hale and their desire for search warrants.

Porter quickly concluded that the warrants wouldn't be a problem. "But let's remember, even if we have proof that he was often in the apartment and presumably was having an affair with the vic, that's a long way from proving that he killed her."

"Understood," said Ginny. "But it sure makes him a strong suspect."

"Agreed."

Because of his having to head back to court, Porter called in one of his assistant prosecutors, who led Joe and Ginny to his cubicle. After getting the particulars, he said he should be able to write up the warrants and get a judge's signature within an hour or so, an hour and a half at the outside.

"That'd be great," said Ginny. "We're going to see him at National Pipe, and then bring him back to the station. I'll give you our fax number so you can fax the warrants over as soon as you have them."

"Will do."

"Great. Thanks. And also, please give our thanks to Mr. Porter. He rushed us out so quickly, we didn't have a chance to properly thank him and say good-bye."

"Not a problem. I'll let him know when he's back from court later this afternoon."

After providing their fax number, Joe and Ginny headed to National Pipe.

CHAPTER 17

Joe and Ginny entered the National Pipe lobby. Joe flashed his badge and said they were there to speak with Mr. Van Hale. The receptionist got all nervous and flustered when she saw the badge. She quickly regained her composure and called Van Hale's administrative assistant.

"Hi, Carol. This is Paula, down in reception."

"Yes, Paula. How can I help you?"

"There are two police officers here to see Mr. Hale."

"Oh, I see. I'll be right down."

"Officers, Mr. Van Hale's executive assistant, Carol Nesbitt, will be right down."

"Thank you. We've met Ms. Nesbitt before. And, by the way, we're detectives, not officers," said Joe.

"I'm sorry. I didn't know."

"Not a problem. Just mentioning it for the future."

Two minutes later, Nesbitt was in the lobby. "Oh, Detectives, I didn't realize it was you. Did you have an appointment with Mr. Van Hale? I'm sure it wasn't on his calendar. Did I mess up?"

"No, not at all, Ms. Nesbitt. We don't have an appointment. Something just came up and we drove right over," said Ginny.

"Well, fortunately, Mr. Van Hale is just meeting with a few of the marketing folks in his office. I'm sure he can break off that meeting for a while to see you."

"Yes, how very fortunate we are," said Joe, unsuccessfully trying to hide his sarcasm.

Nesbitt walked into Van Hale's office and whispered in his ear. Van Hale called a break in the meeting, telling the others that Ms. Nesbitt would call them back when it was time to resume. The meeting participants left, and Nesbitt ushered Joe and Ginny into Van Hale's office. She quickly exited, closing the door behind herself.

"Well, hello, Detectives. Nice to see you again. What can we do for you today? Any progress on identifying Kathryn's killer?"

"We need to talk, Sir," said Joe.

"OK, fine. Take a seat, please. Would you like some coffee? Or a cold drink?"

"No thank you. In fact, we'd rather have our talk downtown at the station house."

"Oh. This must be serious then. What's it about?"

"We'd rather talk about it downtown."

"Are you asking or ordering me downtown? Is something going on that I ought to know about?"

"For now, we're asking, not ordering," said Ginny. "But it's probably in your best interest to accommodate our request."

"What is it? Do I need my attorney?"

"That's totally up to you. It's your right to stop talking until your attorney is present. So why don't we head out now? Then, as you learn more, you can at any time stop and ask for your lawyer."

"OK. Let me grab my coat, and then stop for a minute at Carol's desk on the way out."

"Fine," said Ginny.

"Carol," Van Hale said as they arrived at her desk, "I need to go downtown for a while to help these detectives with something. I'll probably be back too late to finish the marketing meeting, so why don't you reschedule the rest of it for Monday some time. Also, tell Howard that I'll be with these two detectives at the police station. Ask him to go to the station in case I need him to join me."

"OK, I will. Is everything all right, Mr. Van Hale?"

"Oh, definitely. Everything is just fine."

With Joe in the front passenger seat and Van Hale sitting behind Ginny, she drove back to the station and parked. A few minutes later, Joe and Van Hale were sitting in the interrogation room. Shortly thereafter, Ginny joined them with a bottle of water for each of them.

"Now that we're here, can you please tell me what this is all about?"

"Sure. That's what we plan to do," said Joe, who then proceeded to state the where, who and when details into his recorder. "Mr. Van Hale, before we get started I'd like to read you your Miranda rights and have you confirm that you understand them."

"What? Am I a suspect or something?"

"Mr. Van Hale, it's standard procedure," said Ginny. "We read these rights to everyone we talk with here."

"OK. Let's get it over with. The quicker the better."

Joe read the standard statement, which he always carried with him in the front of his notebook, and Van Hale confirmed that he understood his rights.

"Now, can you finally tell me what this is all about?"

"Definitely. It's about Ms. Knox."

"I assumed that much. What specifically about her?"

"How well did you know her?" asked Ginny.

"Quite well. We worked together closely for about four years. You get to know someone pretty well doing that."

"Yes, of course. But I meant on a more, uh, personal level?"

"What do you mean? I don't understand."

"Mr. Van Hale," said Joe, "my partner is trying to be politically correct. What she means is, were you and Ms. Knox romantically involved?"

"What? Of course not," said Van Hale as he leaned forward and glared, first at Joe and then at Ginny. "What the hell are you talking about? I'm a happily married man."

"Sorry, Sir, but we have reason to believe that you and Ms. Knox were seeing each other. Secretly. And I doubt that it was for work, or to play ping pong."

"You're totally mistaken. What so-called reason do you have?"

"Have you ever been in Lennox?"

"Sure. Several times. It has a nice, quaint downtown. And it's only 15 or 20 minutes from here."

"Have you ever eaten in La Pentola in Lennox?"

"I think so. It sounds familiar, but I'm not sure."

"Well, the waitress there sure remembers you," said Joe, as he made a mental note to be sure to check whether the waitress recognized Van Hale's photo.

"Then I guess I must have eaten there. Didn't realize it was a crime, though."

"It's not," said Ginny.

"So?"

"Seems the waitress who remembers you only remembers you dining there in the company of Ms. Knox. Several times."

"Hate to burst your bubble, but I have frequent business meals with members of my staff. Think I'm having affairs with all of them?"

"Not necessarily," said Joe. "Ever been to an apartment at 1311 Jewell Street in Lennox? Apartment C-217, to be more precise."

Just then Steve Klein knocked on the door, opened it and asked Joe or Ginny to step outside. Ginny walked out.

"What is it, Steve?"

"Sorry to interrupt, Ginny, but the guy's lawyer just showed up."

"Damn. We were about to get to the juicy part. Where is he?"

"I've got him sitting next to your desk. Vern's watching him so he doesn't touch or try to read anything."

"OK, thanks."

Ginny walked back to her desk area. A short, chubby and totally bald man stood up. "Hello, I'm Howard Ashley. I'd like to see my client, Philip Van Hale."

"Hello. I'm Detective Harris. Sure, follow me. I'll take you to him."

Ginny and Ashley entered the interrogation room. After quick introductions and hellos, Ashley asked for a few minutes alone with his client. Joe and Ginny left the room, made sure the speaker was off and stood outside the one-way mirror. After about ten minutes, Ashley knocked on the window and waved for the detectives to come back into the room.

"OK if we continue now?" asked Joe.

"Most definitely. Just want to alert you that my client will check with me before he responds to any of your questions."

"Mr. Ashley," said Ginny, "I don't think we've met before. Have you been practicing here for a while?"

"Yes, several years. But I'm a corporate, not criminal, attorney."

"Oh."

"I assure you that I can handle these initial interviews quite well. If, however, you at some point decide to further pursue this foolishness with my client, we would, of course, engage legal counsel who specialize in criminal matters."

"Yes, of course. Let's get started if we can," said Joe. "Just before you arrived, we were asking your client if he'd ever been to apartment C-217 at 1311 Jewell Street in Lennox."

"Yes, and my client won't answer that until you inform us of the significance of that specific apartment and why you're asking."

"Sure. That's where we believe one of his executives, a Kathryn Knox, was murdered," said Ginny.

"I see. And are you asking everyone if they've ever been in that apartment?"

"No," said Joe. "Right now we're only asking your client."

"And why would that be?"

"Mostly 'cause we're curious," said Joe.

"Well, I'm afraid my client won't answer a question asked for such a non-specific reason."

"Not a problem. We already know the answer. We were

just curious how your client would respond — or not respond — to the question."

"Any other questions?"

"Yes, quite a few in fact."

"Mr. Van Hale, for how long have you been having a sexual relationship with Ms. Knox?" asked Ginny.

"As I told you earl—"

"Philip, I told you not to say anything without checking with me first."

"But I—"

"No buts. Either I'm your attorney and you follow my instructions, or you look for another attorney."

"OK. OK, Howard."

"Detectives, my client won't be answering that question."

"Interesting," said Joe. "Not answering really says a lot."

"You're free to think whatever you wish. Now, what else would you like to know?"

"Mr. Van Hale, how would you describe the state of your marriage?" asked Ginny.

"Just fine, as if it's any of your business," blurted out Van Hale before his attorney could cut him off.

"Detectives," said Van Hale's attorney, "any more questions before we call it a day?"

"Sure," said Joe. "Especially if we get answers. For example, where were you at the time of Ms. Knox's death?"

"When exactly would that have been?" asked Ashley.

"Between Friday evening, January 24th, and early Saturday morning on the 25th."

"Howard, can I answer?"

"Go ahead — if you must."

"I'd need to check my agenda at the office to be certain, but I'm fairly sure I was home. Even if my wife and I went out to dinner or something that night, we surely would have been home well before midnight."

"Would you have any witnesses to that?" asked Joe.

"Yeah. My wife, and probably my kids as well."

"Anyone a little more objective?"

"Maybe. If we went to dinner with another couple, or to someone's house. But there wouldn't be any other witnesses to us at three a.m. the next morning."

"So that's less than a solid alibi."

"Hold on, Detective," Ashley interrupted. "I'd guess you wouldn't have any unbiased witnesses to your whereabouts in the middle of the night either, unless you were engaging in some group sex kind of thing. At any rate, unless you want to arrest him, my client and I will be leaving now."

"That's quite all right. Please be sure to notify us if your client plans to leave the state," said Ginny as she and Joe handed their cards to both Van Hale and Ashley. "And thank you for your cooperation, Mr. Van Hale."

"You're welcome. Despite what you may think, I do want to help you in any way I can to find out who the killer is. Ms. Knox meant a lot to us, and will be sorely missed at National Pipe."

And with that, Ashley picked up the water bottle that Van Hale had been drinking from and put it in his coat pocket. Van Hale followed his attorney out the door, down the steps and out of the station.

"Damn," said Ginny. "That mouthpiece sure threw a ringer in things. I felt like we had a chance to make some progress before he showed up and basically cut off the questioning. And he sure was onto our super-tricky attempt to get Van Hale's fingerprints and DNA off his water bottle."

"Yeah. But that's what he gets paid for. If I was a suspect, I'd want a lawyer like that at my side."

"Can't argue with that, Partner. Now what?"

"Four ideas. One, let's get one of the techs in here to try and pick up some of Van Hale's fingerprints from the table or his chair. I doubt if there's any here, but he can also look for a DNA sample."

"Good idea. What're numbers two to four?"

"Show Van Hale's pic to that waitress, so she can hopefully confirm that he's the secret dinner companion. Talk to some of his neighbors. We might get some good insight into the state of their marriage, maybe even some rumors about any hanky-panky. And fourth, I think a visit to Mrs. Van Hale might be illuminating."

"Four good ideas, Joe. You're outdoing yourself."

"I know, but that may mean my idea drawer will be empty for the rest of the day."

"Not a problem. The day's almost over."

Ginny called the Crime Scene Department and arranged for a technician to head over to the interrogation room. Joe informed the other detectives of this, and asked that no one use the room until the technician finished his work. Joe and Ginny then headed out to Joe's car. A short time later, they were in La Pentola, showing four photos, one of which was Van Hale's, to Rosa the waitress. Sure enough, she confirmed that Van Hale was Knox's frequent dinner companion.

Joe and Ginny drove back to Jasper Creek. They happily discussed Rosa's identification of Van Hale. They had an early dinner at a Japanese restaurant and drove to Joe's house, where they watched some TV and went to bed early.

Early Saturday morning, Joe asked Ginny whether there was anything special that she'd like to do over the weekend.

"Sure. I could think of several things. But the freezing weather puts a damper on all of them. So, unless you'd consider flying to Florida for two days, I think we'll just stay here and make believe we're hermits."

"Works for me. We could actually use a little downtime to recharge our batteries. Plus, I can't think of anyone I'd more want to play hermit with than you."

"Joe, I'm amazed how, without even trying, you're so capable of making anything sound sleazy," said Ginny with a smile.

"That's just one of my many unique skills."

And so, hermitting was the adventure for the weekend. Actually, both Joe and Ginny were surprised at how much they enjoyed just staying home and doing nothing.

CHAPTER 18

Joe and Ginny were back at their desks by 7:30 on Monday morning. They checked and confirmed that a Crime Scene technician had spent close to an hour in the interrogation room on Friday, and that, when finished, he had delivered everything he found to Forensics. Ginny called Forensics, but it was too early for anyone other than a few lower-level technicians to be there. Ginny left a message for Sorensen to call her when he got in.

While waiting, Joe and Ginny went to bring the chief up to date.

"Morning, Chief. Want the latest on our dead body in the trunk?" asked Joe.

"Sure. That's always a pleasant topic for starting one's day."

Joe and Ginny sat down in front of the chief's desk and started telling him all that had developed since they last spoke.

"So right now, we're chasing down everything we can about Van Hale, her boss at National Pipe," said Ginny.

"Sure sounds like he could be our perp. Especially if Forensics can confirm he was in that apartment. Will be interesting to see what kind of alibi his wife provides for the night of the murder."

"Right on, Chief," said Joe. "We should hear from Forensics shortly, and then later this morning we're going to visit their neighbors. Then we'll have a little discussion with the wife."

"And we still have LaCroix, her ex-husband, and Lovett, the ex-con from the body shop, as suspects two and three just in case Van Hale doesn't pan out."

"OK. Sounds encouraging. But I'll feel better once you have the perp identified, have a pile of evidence, and he or she is arrested."

"We're with you on that, Chief," said Ginny.

"OK, then," said the chief as looked up at the door, clearly signaling the end of the meeting.

"Just one more thing," said Joe.

"Uh oh, I just knew things were going too well."

"Nothing like that, Chief. It's just that it looks like, based on what the Crime Scene crew found, the murder took place in that Lennox apartment. Ginny and I really don't want to be pulled off this case. We feel like we're making a lot of progress now, and we don't want to risk any hiccups if we have to transfer everything to the Lennox guys. I mean, except for the murder scene itself, all the key characters, including the vic and the probable perp, live and work here in Jasper Creek. We don't care who gets the official credit for the case, we just want to continue to run it."

"Understood. And I don't blame you. Let me give Chief Zanelli over there a call. He and I go way back together. I'll see if we can work something out."

"OK, great. Thanks, Chief."

"Yeah, thanks," added Ginny. "We're outta your hair now."

Silent nods, and Joe and Ginny left the chief's office.

Back at their desks, a pink slip of paper indicated that Ginny had missed the return phone call from Sorensen. Ginny called him back.

"Hello, Forensics. Sorensen speaking. How can I be of help?"

"Hi, Christen. Ginny Harris. Sorry I missed your call a few minutes ago."

"Not a problem. I was calling to tell you what we found from the stuff we got from your interrogation room."

"Great. Let me put you on speaker. Joe's right here with me."

"Fine. Hello, Joe."

"Hi, Christen. Whadda we know?"

"A few things. Like, a helluva lot of people have been in that little room. Not too many different prints on the table and chair where you said your suspect was sitting. I guess the department does too good a job of cleaning. But there were a lot of different prints on the door and door frame. Guess the cleaning crew skips there."

"What else?"

"Several of the people who've been in there are folks on the job. And that includes you two."

"Wow. That's just amazing information. Who would have ever guessed?" asked Joe, as he smiled at Ginny. "But seriously, Christen, anything that ties to the Knox murder?"

"Yup. I was just about to get to that. One set of prints, or more accurately, a few sets of the same print, in the interrogation room match several sets that we found in the apartment in Lennox. And also in Knox's car, which had been towed in from that parking lot in Lennox."

"Fantastic!" said Ginny as she high-fived Joe. "Whose prints are they?"

"No idea."

"Damn."

"We know they definitely match each other, but they're not in any of the databases. We checked the prints in the system for that ex-con Lovett and for that LaCroix guy, but neither is a match. We'll only be able to identify the person if you bring one of his or her prints to us, along with his or her name."

"We get that," said Ginny. "It's still a big step forward for us. Any usable DNA samples?"

"No. Nada. Sorry."

"No problem. We appreciate you expediting the fingerprint stuff. What you found is real helpful. Now we gotta bring you a few named prints for comparison."

"Sounds good. Take care."

"Bye."

After hanging up, Ginny said, "It's not one hundred percent sure, of course, but I'd be shocked if the common prints aren't Van Hale's."

"I agree. He's probably the only one to have left fingerprints in that room with a connection to Knox. Except, of course, for LaCroix, and possibly Lovett. And neither Lovett's prints from his earlier arrest or LaCroix's from his earlier scuffles are a match."

"Yeah, my money's on Van Hale."

"Now what?"

"What say we grab a couple of uniforms and execute the search warrant for Van Hale's house? Once the uniforms start the search, you and I can have a little chat, perhaps over tea, with the Mrs."

"Sounds like a plan to me."

Ginny arranged with the Patrol sergeant for three uniformed officers to meet Joe and Ginny in the parking lot in a half-hour. Ginny checked Van Hale's home address, and entered it into the GPS system in her cell phone.

Thirty minutes later, Joe, with Ginny sitting next to him, was leading two patrol cars carrying a total of three uniformed officers to Van Hale's house in the northwest section of town.

About 20 minutes later, they all pulled up and parked in front of a large, Georgian house — two stories with four white columns across the front; red brick, with white trim around the windows and front door, a black front door and black shutters at each window. A white picket fence surrounded the property, with a gray brick walkway from the street to a short flight of steps leading to the front door. A driveway went around the right side of the house, presumably to a garage in the rear. There were several attractive bushes along the front of the house. Although the lawn was covered with snow, Ginny assumed it was meticulously cared for during the growing season. *When Joe next asks me what I'd like our future house to be like, I can just refer him back here.*

Joe and Ginny led the way to the front door. Joe knocked, and a minute later the door was opened by a tall, attractive, bleach-blonde middle-aged woman, dressed as if she were expecting some women friends over for lunch.

"Yes, may I help you?"

"Mrs. Van Hale?" asked Ginny. "We're Detectives Harris and McFarland."

"Yes. Is anything wrong? My husband? Our boys?"

"No, not that we're aware of. May we come in?"

"Yes, of course."

Mrs. Van Hale, the two detectives and the three patrolmen all fit easily into the large foyer.

"Mrs. Van Hale," said Ginny, "we have a warrant to search your house and car. I assume your husband's car is at his office, not here?"

As Joe handed the warrant to Mrs. Van Hale, she asked, "Why? What is this about?"

"It's all explained in the warrant," said Joe.

"May I contact my husband first? Or our attorney?"

"Yes, of course."

Mrs. Van Hale took a cell phone out of a pocket in her skirt and called her husband. After a short discussion, she hung up and spoke to Joe and Ginny. "My husband said I shouldn't let you do anything until I hear from our attorney. He's calling him now."

"As a courtesy, we're willing to wait a few minutes for you and your lawyer to talk. But if it takes too long, we'll have to proceed."

Less than a minute later, Mrs. Van Hale's phone rang, and she was speaking with their attorney.

"Detectives, our attorney, Howard Ashley, would like to speak with one of you."

Joe put his hand out, and Mrs. Van Hale passed him the phone. Joe and Ashley spoke for a few minutes, and then hung up.

"Ginny, I agreed that you'd take photos of the warrant

and text them to Ashley," said Joe as he handed the phone to Ginny. Joe then shrugged, explaining that Ginny was the technical wizard of their team.

Five minutes later, Ashley called and asked to speak with Joe.

"Detective, the warrant seems to be in order. I can't imagine why you're going to these crazy extremes, but that's your business. It's OK to proceed with the search. But I don't want you questioning Mrs. Van Hale without my being present. I am her attorney, as well as attorney for Mr. Van Hale and National Pipe."

"Understood. We were going to talk with her here, but why don't you meet us at the station at about two instead? We'll bring her there with us, then you can drive her back here when we're done."

"OK. Let me speak with her now and explain everything."

Joe handed the phone back to Mrs. Van Hale, who was told of the decisions reached and instructed not to answer any questions without Ashley at her side.

With that, Joe, Ginny and the three officers began a careful, thorough search of the house, the garage and Mrs. Van Hale's car. They weren't sure what they were looking for, other than anything linking Van Hale and Knox. Ginny tested all of the shoes in Van Hale's closet for blood residue. The left shoe of one pair tested positive. Ginny put that pair into an evidence bag, filled out the information on the outside of the bag and signed it. She then wrote out a receipt for the shoes. An hour and a half later they were finished, not having found anything other than the shoes and a few business papers with both Van Hale's and Knox's names on them.

Joe and Ginny released the two Patrol officers who were sharing a patrol car, and Joe asked the third officer to stay with Mrs. Van Hale while Joe and Ginny ran a quick errand. Before they left, Ginny explained to Mrs. Van Hale that they were taking one pair of her husband's shoes with them for further analysis, and she gave Mrs. Van Hale the receipt she had written earlier.

Once in Joe's car, Ginny asked, "What's this important errand we have to run?"

"I'll give you a hint. The first three letters are L-U-N."

"Oh, you sneak. I bet the last two letters are C-H."

"Boy, I can't get anything past you."

Joe pulled into the first McDonald's he saw, and the two detectives were soon munching away at a quiet corner table.

"I hope the blood on that shoe turns out to be the victim's. Too bad we didn't find anything else incriminating," said Ginny.

"Yeah. But we knew it was a long shot. What's really bad is that Ashley's going to mess up our interview with the wife."

"Well, he is doing his job."

"I know. But why does he have to do it so well?"

"Maybe because lots of money lets you buy the best lawyers."

"Yeah, there's probably something to that, Ginny."

"But I did learn something important."

"What's that?"

"When you ask me what kind of house I'd like us to get,

I can just say Van Hale's. The outside's beautiful, and the inside's even better. High quality, attractive, efficient and cozy. It was even in what looked to be a great neighborhood."

"I agree. But it's probably umpteen times what we can afford."

"We could go with a smaller version. No way we need five bedrooms. Plus, I don't think we need a formal living room *and* a casual family room — one or the other's enough."

"It did seem nice, but I think even a smaller version is way up there in price."

"Well, we won't know 'til we start shopping."

"True enough. But now it's time to finish our important errand and go pick the wife up."

"Right you are."

CHAPTER 19

Less than an hour later, the two detectives and Mrs. Van Hale were in the same interrogation room her husband had been in on Friday. While waiting for her attorney to arrive, Joe stated the required information into his recorder and read Mrs. Van Hale her rights. Howard Ashley arrived a few minutes later and joined them.

"OK, let's get started now if we can," said Joe.

"Sure thing," said Ashley. "And, Barbara, do not say anything without checking with me first. If you and I need to discuss anything at any time, I'm sure the detectives will be kind enough to step outside."

"OK," said Mrs. Van Hale.

"Mrs. Van Hale," said Ginny, "did you know the victim, Kathryn Knox?"

Ashley nodded his head when Van Hale looked his way. "Yes, of course. Over the years, there were several events involving Philip and his team, and spouses were sometimes included. The annual Christmas party, occasional dinners with the board and so on. She was even at our home a few times, along with some of the other executives, for cocktail parties or dinners that we hosted."

"And were those the only occasions during which you were with Ms. Knox?"

"Yes, that's correct. I saw her a couple of times a year at these events. Oh, and I did see her occasionally when I went to visit Philip at his office. I obviously knew her, but we weren't by any means friends."

"Were you enemies? Or rivals?" asked Joe.

"Enemies? Not at all. We just weren't friends. And rivals? What do you mean? Rivals about what?"

"I don't know. That's why I'm asking you. She and your husband did spend a lot of after-hours time together."

"Those so-called after-hours times involved work. She was Philip's CFO, and they often had to spend time working evenings and weekends. That's what executives have to do. What are you implying?"

"Mrs. Van Hale, are you saying it never entered your mind that there might be something other than work going on between them? Especially once Ms. Knox got divorced."

"Howard, do I have to listen to this kind of thing? It's very upsetting. And totally unfounded."

"Detectives, I suggest we move along to another topic."

"Sure," said Joe. "Mrs. Van Hale, where were you and where was your husband the night Ms. Knox was killed?"

"I have no idea. I don't even remember what night she was killed."

"It was Friday, the 25th of last month."

"Well, I still don't know without checking my calendar, which is at home. We could have been home that evening, or gone out someplace given that it was a Friday. Or Philip might have had to work late, or had a meeting or dinner that evening. Or he could have been returning home from a business trip."

"Wow, that's quite a range of possibilities," said Joe.

"I'm sure we can narrow it down significantly once I

look at my calendar, and Philip, or his assistant, Carol, checks his work agenda."

"Did you know that your husband and Ms. Knox often had dinner in a restaurant in Lennox?"

"No, but so what? Philip usually had business dinners a few times a week."

"And did you know that he was often seen entering a nearby apartment that was rented by Ms. Knox, or by your husband, or by both of them?"

"What? No. You must be mistaken. I know for a fact that she lived in a house right here in Jasper Creek. And I'm sure I'd know if Philip had been renting an apartment someplace."

"Mrs. Van Hale, how would you describe your marriage?" asked Ginny.

"What? Just fine. What are you getting at?"

"Just trying to understand things. Were you two happily married? Did your husband have any reason to, ah, stray? Any unfaithful situations in the past?"

"Detective, I think that's—" Mrs. Van Hale began.

"Hold it right there, Detectives," Ashley broke in. "I think we've gone far enough. If you don't have any more questions relevant to Ms. Knox's murder, Mrs. Van Hale and I will be on our way."

"Not a problem," said Joe. "But I'm sure we'll be in touch with more questions as we progress in our investigation."

"Fine. When you do, please contact me and not Mrs. Van Hale."

"As you wish," said Joe.

Ashley escorted Van Hale out of the room and to his

car so he could drive her home. Joe and Ginny remained sitting in the interrogation room.

Banging his fist on the table, Joe said, "Damn. I bet we could have gotten some useful info from her if that damn lawyer wasn't with her."

"I agree. But it is what it is. She did seem to get a little spooked when we pressed her on their marriage, his possibly screwing around and his being in that apartment."

"Sure did. We need to do some more digging. And we have to get his fingerprints in a way that we can certify they're his, so Forensics can confirm for sure that he was in that apartment."

"You made it sound so convincing that even I half-believed we had firm evidence he was in there."

"We will. And my guess is that the vic was not his first outside-of-marriage plaything."

"Oh, Joe, you say that so delicately."

"Well, of course. I'm a cultured and sensitive gentleman."

"How about we not split hairs? Let's just agree that you're a man," said Ginny with a half-smile.

"Works for me, Partner."

Joe walked back to his desk, returned two phone calls and started to clean up some paperwork. Ginny joined him after dropping Van Hale's shoes off at Forensics.

"Got a couple of minutes?"

Joe and Ginny looked up, both surprised that someone as overweight as the chief could sneak up on them so silently.

"Uh, yeah. Sure," said Ginny.

"Come on," said the chief as he pivoted and headed back toward his office.

Joe and Ginny looked at each other, and Ginny gave the slightest shrug. They both got up and hurried after the chief.

When all three were seated in the chief's office, the chief jumped right in. "I just hung up from talking with my old friend, Chief Zanelli, over in Lennox."

"And?" asked Joe, with some trepidation in his voice.

"I think we agreed on a reasonable accommodation. But that's up to you two."

"Doesn't sound too great so far. What's the deal?"

"As you know, with the crime almost certainly taking place in their jurisdiction, it should officially become their case. Not much we can do about that."

"Doesn't sound like the best deal I ever heard of," said Joe.

"Just hang onto your pants. Let me finish before you start moaning and groaning."

"OK. Sorry, Chief. Go ahead."

"Fortunately, it's in the same county, so nothing changes with regard to the county prosecutor or Forensics."

"Yeah, but what about Ginny and—?"

"Hold on, Joe. You said you'd let me finish."

"You're right. Go ahead."

"Zanelli agreed that you two could continue leading the investigation, but only on two conditions."

"Here it comes. I bet this'll be a doozy."

"Joe, let's give the chief a chance to lay it out."

"Thank you, Ginny," said the chief. "Like I said, there're two conditions. First, you need to coordinate things very closely with the two detectives he's planning to assign to the case. You need to keep them fully informed. Joe, although it's only an informal arrangement, you need to treat it like some of the joint task forces you were on in Chicago. If he gets one complaint from his detectives, the deal's off and they take over the case."

"That doesn't sound so bad. Does it, Joe?" said Ginny.

"I guess it's better than nothing. What's the second condition?"

"If he starts getting pressure about this from his boss, or if he starts to feel that progress is being made too slowly, or even if he starts feeling uncomfortable about being responsible for this case but basically not in control over how it's being handled, all bets are off."

"Just great!" said Joe. "That's basically saying he can change his mind whenever he feels like it."

"That's right. He's cooperating with us now, but is reserving the right to change his mind whenever."

"Wonderful! What a fantastic deal!" said Joe as he started to stand up.

"Oh, you're very welcome, Joe," said the chief. "I'm glad to see how much you appreciate what I was able to arrange."

"Yeah, Chief. Thanks," said Joe.

"Yes, thanks," added Ginny.

"He's probably talking with his two detectives now. He said he'd have them call you two, so the four of you can work out your game plan."

"OK," said Joe, as he and Ginny got up to return to their desks.

"Shit!" said Joe as he banged the side of his fist on his desk.

"Joe. Take it easy. Do you really think it's that bad?"

"Hell, yes. Even worse than that."

"But, Joe."

"Ginny, you never served on a JTF. I have. Several times. And they all were varying degrees of terrible. Especially in the first month or two, when everybody's jockeying for position. Hell, it's like a bunch of male elks fighting to be leader of the harem of female elks."

"Maybe it'll be different this time."

"Doubt it. And we gotta be super sure to tell our so-called partners every time we're going to take a leak. They have total power over us. One complaint to their chief, and we're off the case. And we have to hope that their chief doesn't just wake up one morning and change his mind."

"Let's at least wait to meet our partners before we start hating them."

"Fair enough. But you'll see. Let's wrap it up and get out of here. I've had it for today."

A few minutes later, they were on their way to Joe's house.

Following a dinner of chicken breasts and packaged vegetables from Joe's freezer, Ginny started to reopen discussion about the case. But, based on Joe's still-glum view of the arrangement, she quickly chose silence over more complaining from Joe.

Around eight o'clock, Ginny's cell phone rang.

"Yes, Detective. Thanks for calling. Yes, our chief filled us in on the arrangement. Tomorrow morning? Hold on, let me check with my partner." Turning to Joe with her hand over her cell phone, Ginny said, "Joe, it's one of the Lennox detectives. He's suggesting that the four of us have breakfast tomorrow to get to know each other and go over the case."

"Sure. Fine. Might as well get it over with. I assume we have to drive to Lennox. So they have home court advantage."

"In fact, he offered to meet us here in JC."

"Wow. Miracles never cease. OK, let's do it."

Ginny arranged for Joe and her to meet with the two Lennox detectives at the Main Street Diner at seven the next morning. She gave the Lennox detective the diner's address, thanked him for calling and hung up.

"Joe, see? Not too bad. He sounded quite reasonable."

"We'll find out soon enough tomorrow."

Virtually no more communications took place that night. Joe and Ginny watched two TV shows in silence and then headed to bed.

CHAPTER 20

Joe and Ginny left Joe's house about 6:40 the next morning and were at the Main Street Diner a few minutes before seven. They went in, grabbed a large booth near the rear and ordered two coffees while they waited. At about 7:05, the two Lennox detectives arrived, introduced themselves and sat down.

William Fernald, who stated very firmly that he was fine with William or Will, but did not want to be called Bill, was clearly the leader of the Lennox pair. Tall, slightly overweight, and with long, wavy gray hair, Fernald looked to be in his mid-50s. Juan Rodriguez, short, very muscular and probably in his early 30s, indicated that he'd been promoted to detective about six months earlier and that this would be his first homicide case. His enthusiasm and excitement reminded Joe of a little kid going to see his first baseball game.

"Joe, Ginny. Before we dive into the case, I want to clear the air," said Fernald. "I've been where you two are now. And it sucks. No two ways about it. You caught the case, you did all the initial work and now you're told to drop it, or at least share it all with us. I hated that when it happened to me, so I know how you feel. But that's how the cookie crumbled, or, more to the point, how the vic died. Unless there's evidence that moves the scene back to your jurisdiction, we're the folks officially in charge. End of that part."

"Yeah, we know. Only too well," said Joe.

"But let me finish. Juan and I already discussed this. So long as you keep us fully informed, and I do mean fully, and we feel like you at least give our ideas a fair hearing, we're fine with you two informally calling the shots."

"Do you really mean that, Will?" asked Joe.

"Totally. We want to be there for the arrest, but we have no problem with you guys getting credit for the collar."

"That's fine," said Joe. "We're not hung up on who gets the credit. It's more that nothing falls to the floor during the hand-off."

"OK," said Ginny. "Sounds like we're off to a good start. Let's order, then Joe and I can bring you up to speed on the case."

Not surprisingly, everyone ordered the Deuces Special — two eggs, two bacon strips, two pancakes and two pieces of toast. Plus, of course, coffees for Fernald and Rodriguez and refills for Ginny and Joe.

Joe and Ginny took turns talking and eating. Over the next 45 minutes, they gave Fernald and Rodriguez a detailed summary of the case, what Joe and Ginny had done and found, and Joe and Ginny's current list of possible perps — from Van Hale to LaCroix to Lovett. Ginny mentioned their plan to visit Van Hale's executive assistant, and invited the two Lennox detectives to join them.

"Thanks, Ginny, but I think we'll pass," said Fernald. "Four detectives all at once might be a little overwhelming. But we appreciate you informing and inviting us. With that kind of communication and cooperation, we shouldn't have any problem working together."

"Glad to hear that," said Ginny. "We'll let you know what we learn."

"One other thing," said Joe. "Our chief made it clear that, despite our playing nice with you guys, your chief could end our involvement whenever he starts to feel uncomfortable — pressure from upstairs, thinking we're making too little progress or whatever. Should we be worried about that?"

"As long as we're working well together," said Fernald, "I don't think so. Our chief always likes to be sure he's got an out to anything he agrees to. Not sure if he once got burned badly, or if he's just honing his skills to become a politician. But, unless the four of us screw up badly, I don't think it's an issue."

"Very glad to hear that," said Joe.

Each detective left $10 on the table, enough for their breakfast and a more than generous tip. Fernald and Rodriguez headed back to Lennox, and Joe and Ginny headed for National Pipe to talk with Carol Nesbitt, Van Hale's executive assistant and Knox's former executive assistant.

"Joe, I think that went very well. They seem to be pleasant and reasonable. We should be able to work well with them."

Glancing quickly at Ginny so he could focus on the road, Joe said, "OK, I admit it. It did go better than I expected."

"Maybe it's the nice people who live around here vs. those cold city folks in places like Chicago."

"Yeah. Maybe. We'll see. Can't tell for sure until we have a real conflict. Then everyone's true colors come out."

"OK. We'll wait and see. But I'm optimistic."

"Wouldn't expect anything else from Miss Optimist of the Year," said Joe with a smile.

Joe and Ginny arrived at National Pipe a few minutes before nine. The receptionist called Nesbitt, and she met the detectives in the lobby a few minutes later.

"Good morning, Detectives. How may I help you?"

"We've got a few more questions," said Ginny. "Is there someplace private we can sit down for a few minutes?"

"Sure. Follow me." Nesbitt led Joe and Ginny into one of three minuscule offices right off the lobby. The three of them sat down around a small table, and Nesbitt explained, "These offices are for sales people who visit. It lets them meet with our purchasing or technical folks without giving them access to our whole plant area. We're often working on things that we want to keep confidential."

"I see. Ms. Nesbitt, do you know if Mr. Van Hale and Ms. Knox were working together the evening she was killed?"

"Don't know, but let me take a look." Nesbitt swung the computer monitor and keyboard that were on the table around to face her, entered her user name and password and was soon looking at Van Hale's and Knox's calendars. "Neither of them had anything scheduled that evening. But it's possible that something came up last minute, and they wound up working together. That often happened."

"Did you see them together that evening?"

"No. When I left around five that evening they were working alone in their own offices."

"Did they often work together in the evenings?" asked Ginny.

"Well, I wouldn't say often, but it did happen fairly frequently."

"About how often?" asked Joe.

"Oh, let's see. Maybe one or two times a week, on average?"

"And was it usually marked in their calendars?"

"Once in a while, but usually not."

"And did it happen a lot more often with Ms. Knox than with the other executives?" asked Joe.

"Um, yes, now that you mention it. Are you implying that something was going on between them?"

"I'm not implying anything. But do you think there was? Or could have been?"

"Yikes. That never entered my mind. I'm not aware of anything like that, but, of course, I can't be certain that it wasn't happening."

"Could Ms. Knox have been involved with anyone else here?" asked Joe.

"No. I'm sure not. She was always friendly with the others, but she kept her distance. Especially after she got divorced. I think a few of the single executives asked her out once or twice, but she always said no. That she didn't want to mix business and pleasure. She never told me that, but that was the word going around."

"Ms. Nesbitt," said Joe, "I don't want to put words in your mouth, but is this a fair summary of what you've been saying? You have no reason to think she was seeing or dating anyone from work, but if it turned out she was, Mr. Van Hale would be the only likely person."

"It sounds sleazy when you say it that way, but yes, that's pretty much right on."

"Ms. Nesbitt, is Mr. Van Hale in this morning?" asked Ginny.

"No. He's on his way to Pittsburgh to meet with a major customer later today."

"Is he driving?" asked Joe.

"No. That is, he's going by car, but he's not doing the driving. He's going with our sales and marketing vp, and he's the one driving."

"And Mr. Van Hale's car?"

"It's right outside in the parking lot. He left it there when they met early this morning."

"I see. OK if we have our technicians check Mr. Van Hale's car? They can do it right here in the lot."

"Uh. Sure. I don't see why not. As long as they're done by later this afternoon, when Mr. Van Hale will need the car to drive home. But I better check with Mr. Ashley, the company's and Mr. Van Hale's attorney, first."

"Go ahead. Not a problem. Mr. Ashley has already seen this search warrant," Joe said as he handed the warrant to Nesbitt. "I'm sure he'll be OK with the search."

Nesbitt called Ashley. After a brief discussion, she hung up and told the detectives that it was indeed OK to search the car.

"Fine. Thanks. We'll have our techs ask for you when they get here," said Joe.

"OK. That'll be fine. Anything else I can help you with?"

"No. That's it for now. Thanks for your help."

Back in Joe's car, Ginny called the station to arrange for Crime Scene to get a few technicians to Van Hale's car that morning to capture his, and anyone else's, fingerprints.

Joe parked in the PD lot, and, without even discussing it, the two detectives started walking toward Sancho's Taco shop.

Forty-five minutes later, they were on their way back to the station.

"Joe, I'll meet you upstairs in a few. I want to check in with Forensics and get an update. And light a fire under them if need be."

"And you think your delicate fire-lighting is likely to be more successful than the barn fire I'd light up?"

"Your words, not mine. But yeah, that says it pretty well."

"I'd argue pretty hard with you. If I didn't think you were right," said Joe while chuckling.

Twenty minutes later, Ginny joined Joe at their desks.

"So, Miss Fire-Lighter?"

"I got some good info, but I did need to light a little fire to put a rush on the rest."

"And?"

"Van Hale's shoes are a perfect match. The blood on the one shoe matches, and the tread size, design and wear perfectly match the pattern in the mud on the floor. No question he was there at the time of, or at least soon after, her murder."

"Finally, some good, solid evidence that supports us."

"They were also able to get some good fingerprints from Van Hale's car. Nice to know those folks went right at it while we had a leisurely lunch at Sancho's."

"Whose were they?"

"They assume, probably rightly so, that the most common print in the car is Van Hale's. But until we get them a print that we know for sure is his, they can't definitively conclude that. There were also several other prints in the car, but they haven't had a chance to try to identify them yet. That's where my fire-lighting had to come in. But the important piece of news is that the prints from the car that most likely are Van Hale's match some of the prints from the apartment in Lennox."

"Aha," said Joe. "So, it increasingly looks like they did more than work and eat dinners together. If we get them one of his prints, we'll have more than enough proof that he's been to that apartment."

"Right you are. We should get a warrant for his prints, and let's go for a DNA sample as well. We can exercise it tonight, when he's back from Pittsburgh, or tomorrow morning."

"Works for me. Let's walk over to Porter's office and get it."

Joe and Ginny walked to the prosecutor's office. Porter was in court all day, so they dealt with Assistant Prosecutor Gantz. Joe and Ginny provided detailed background information and the reasons for suspecting Van Hale. Gantz indicated that obtaining a warrant shouldn't be difficult, and that she'd fax it to Joe and Ginny as soon as she had it signed by a judge.

Joe and Ginny returned to their desks. Less than two hours later they had the faxed warrant. Ginny called Nesbitt and learned that Van Hale was expected back in the office around four or 4:15.

At 3:45, Joe and Ginny arrived at National Pipe. Nesbitt

met them in the lobby and escorted them to Van Hale's office, where they sat awaiting his return.

A few minutes before 4:30, Van Hale walked in. "Hello, Detectives. Carol told me that you were here waiting for me. How can I help you?"

"Mr. Van Hale," said Ginny, "we're here to collect your fingerprints and a DNA sample."

"Huh? Why? Do you think I had anything to do with Kathryn's death? That's crazy."

"Mr. Van Hale, please don't overreact. This is rather routine. The more people we can clear as suspects or possible suspects, the better the chance we have of identifying the guilty party."

"And if I refuse?"

"You'll wind up going downtown with us. Mr. Van Hale, we took the liberty of obtaining a warrant for these samples just in case," said Joe as he took the warrant out of his pocket, unfolded it and handed it to Van Hale.

Van Hale spent a few minutes reading the warrant and then said, "OK. I'm not a lawyer, but I've dealt with far too many legal documents over the years. This looks legitimate. Let's go ahead and get this over with."

"Wise decision. Thanks," said Ginny.

Ginny then opened the small case she was carrying. She put on disposable gloves, took finger and palm prints from Van Hale and then swabbed the inside of his cheek for a DNA sample. She carefully put the prints and swab in two separate evidence bags, filled out the information, signed the outside of the bags and put everything back into the case.

Joe and Ginny thanked Van Hale, said their good-byes

to him and Nesbitt and headed back to the station. Joe waited in the car while Ginny delivered the fingerprints and DNA sample to Forensics.

Ten minutes later, Ginny was back in Joe's car.

"Joe, I hate to be a party pooper, but I suggest we go our separate ways tonight. I haven't been to my condo in ages, and I'm sure it needs a good cleaning. Plus, a good night's sleep wouldn't hurt either of us."

"I understand. No problem. I'll drop you off, and then pick you up again in the morning. Say eight?"

"Eight'll be fine. And thanks for understanding."

CHAPTER 21

Ginny was back in Forensics at 8:30 the next morning.

"Good morning, Christen."

"Morning, Ginny. Hope you're not here already about the prints and DNA you dropped off late yesterday."

"Just wanted to be sure you knew about them. Hopefully, you can fast-track them."

"I do know about them, and I am fast-tracking them."

"Oh. Great."

"Go ahead, Ginny. You can ask. Don't be shy."

"Ask what?"

"Oh, Christen dear," said Sorensen in a falsetto voice, "when do you think we'll have the results?" And then, switching back to his normal voice, "Oh, thanks for asking, Ginny. Should have something regarding the prints in an hour or so."

"That's great. Thanks. Call me as soon as you have something."

"It was good you said that, Ginny. Otherwise, I probably would have just sat on the results for a week and then mailed them to you."

"Very funny. But seriously, thanks."

An hour later, Ginny got the call from Sorensen. "Sure enough, Ginny, the prints are definitive proof that Van Hale was in the apartment in Lennox. In theory, someone else could have been wearing his shoes. But it's pretty doubtful that anyone could have borrowed his fingerprints. And, no surprise, the most common prints from his car do belong to Van Hale. We're still working to identify some of the others."

"Great. That's a big step forward for us. Let me know if you learn anything from the DNA sample."

"Will do."

As Ginny was hanging up her phone, Joe said, "Your side of the call made it sound rather promising. What's the scoop?"

"Good news. The fingerprints confirm that Van Hale was in the apartment."

"Super. Let's go get the bum and bring him back here for a little sweating."

"Hold on, Joe. You're forgetting that this is actually Lennox's case, not ours. As a minimum, we ought to bring Fernald and Rodriguez up to date. See if they agree with the next step. If they do, they may want to be the ones who sweat him."

"You're right, Ginny. Why don't you call them and set up a meeting? In the meantime, I'll mosey down the hall and give the chief an update."

"Sounds good to me."

While Ginny called Detective Fernald and arranged for Joe and Ginny to meet Fernald and Rodriguez for lunch at Sancho's at noon, Joe spent about ten minutes bringing the chief up to date. It must have been a good day for the chief. He actually thanked Joe for playing nice with the Lennox detectives.

Joe and Ginny got to Sancho's around 11:50 and found

Fernald and Rodriguez already sitting at a table for four, right next to the large front window.

"Hi, Detectives," said Joe. "Didn't expect you guys to already be here."

"Guess we were hungrier than we thought. Although, actually, we left a little extra time as we weren't sure if we'd hit any traffic."

"We're the same way," said Ginny. "We'd much rather be early than late."

"Sounds like that's at least one thing we can all agree on."

"Well, let's order. Then we'll bring you up to date on where things stand, and on what we think the next steps should be," said Joe. "We'll see if that's also something we can all agree on."

Joe and Ginny went with soft tacos and diet sodas. Fernald and Rodriguez studied the menu intensely, then wound up duplicating Joe and Ginny's orders. The waitress brought a large bowl of tortillas, along with two bowls of salsa — one mild and one extra spicy — and four Diet Cokes.

While munching on the tortillas and salsa and awaiting their tacos, Joe and Ginny brought the two Lennox detectives up to date on what they'd found, especially the fingerprint proof that Van Hale had been in that apartment.

The Lennox detectives agreed with the plan to bring Van Hale in for further questioning. But with one twist.

"Don't take this the wrong way, but I think we should do that in Lennox, rather than you doing it here in Jasper Creek."

"Oh. Why's that?" asked Joe as he gave a sideways glance to Ginny.

"A couple of reasons," said Fernald. "First of all, the crime was committed in Lennox and it is officially our case. Although we're fine with you taking the lead and doing most everything, we do have to take an occasional action ourselves. If nothing else, for appearance's sake for our boss. Secondly, bringing him to Lennox may add to Van Hale's worry and stress. It makes the interrogation seem bigger and more important than just doing it locally."

"And there's another good reason," added Rodriguez.

"Namely?" asked Joe.

"We never met his attorney, and we were never told to question him only with his attorney present. If we're lucky, we might get some quality time with Van Hale before he yells for his lawyer."

"I must say, all your arguments seem reasonable. I'm OK with you taking the lead on this. Joe?"

"Yeah, that'll be OK. But we'd better accompany you when you go to pick him up. This is Jasper Creek and not Lennox, you know."

"Works for me," said Fernald.

While finishing their meal, the four detectives talked through some of the logistical details of picking up Van Hale for questioning.

Following lunch, they walked over to the county prosecutor's office.

"I'm glad we're in the same county. Lot less complicated, right?" said Rodriguez.

They requested an arrest warrant for Van Hale,

provided all their evidence and the other required information, and asked that the warrant be faxed to Fernald and Rodriguez's offices. The two Lennox detectives then followed Joe and Ginny to National Pipe. They were soon met in the lobby by Nesbitt and led upstairs to Van Hale's office.

"Hello, Detectives. Back again. How can I help you? Looks like you brought some reinforcements with you today."

Joe introduced Van Hale and the two Lennox detectives to each other. He then explained that the Lennox detectives wanted to take him to Lennox for further questioning about Knox's death.

"And if I don't agree to go with them?"

"We'll quickly get an arrest warrant. We'll arrest you and hold you here in Jasper Creek until Lennox files an extradition request. So you'll still wind up there, but after wasting several hours in our jail. Also, it will make it look like you have something to hide," responded Joe.

"Well, you make it sound like I don't really have much of a choice. So, let's do it and get it over with. I have nothing to hide."

The two Lennox detectives drove Van Hale to the Lennox PD and joined him in a small interrogation room. Unbeknownst to Van Hale, Joe and Ginny had also driven to Lennox and were standing outside the interrogation room, behind the one-way mirror.

Inside the interrogation room, Rodriguez turned on a small recorder and stated the date, time, place and occupants of the room. Fernald then read Van Hale his Miranda rights.

"Before we get started, may I ask a question?" said Van Hale.

"Sure," said Rodriguez. "But it remains to be seen whether or not we answer you."

"OK. Why are you guys involved? And why isn't this taking place in Jasper Creek?"

"Technically, that's two questions, not one. But we'll let you slide on that. Whadda ya think, Juan?"

Rodriguez nodded his head.

"Mr. Van Hale," said Fernald, "we're here because it turns out that Ms. Knox was killed in Lennox. Despite both her and you living and working in Jasper Creek, that makes this a Lennox crime and we, therefore, are the agency directing the investigation."

"Killed here in Lennox? Where? How? How do you know?"

"Sorry, but you've used up all your allowable questions. It's now our turn to ask, and yours to answer."

The two detectives started by asking Van Hale almost the identical questions Joe and Ginny had previously asked. Not surprisingly, Van Hale gave the same answers he had given to Joe and Ginny. The detectives also asked a few new questions.

"Mr. Van Hale, any idea how your fingerprints could be all over that apartment if you were never there?" asked Fernald.

"No idea. Maybe there's some way someone could've picked up my fingerprints with tape or something, and then transferred them to another location."

"Yup. A lot of things are theoretically possible, even if extremely unlikely."

"Well, you tell me then."

"Happy to," said Fernald. "Your fingerprints are all over the crime scene because you've been in that apartment. Several times, in fact."

"But—"

"Mr. Van Hale, we have eyewitnesses identifying you as the male who frequented that apartment with Ms. Knox."

"Even you know how unreliable eyewitnesses are."

"Mr. Van Hale, are you and your wife happily married? How many times has she discovered you being unfaithful? Does she know about you and Ms. Knox?"

"That's it. I'm done. I want my lawyer here before I answer any more questions."

"Not a problem," said Fernald. "We're done with our questions for now. But there is one other thing."

"What's that?"

"Mr. Van Hale, please stand up and put your hands behind your back. You're under arrest for the second-degree murder of Kathryn Knox. And for obstruction of justice. By relocating the victim's body."

"What! Are you crazy? I want my lawyer. Now."

"We need to process you first. Then you can call your lawyer. He'll be able to find you without any difficulty. You'll be right here. Let's go."

Fernald and Rodriguez led Van Hale out of the interrogation room and down the hall for fingerprinting and processing.

Still in the observation area outside of the interrogation room, Ginny said, "Wow. Those guys don't fool around. We wanted to sweat Van Hale. He must be soaking wet by now."

"For sure. Let's go sit by their desks until they're finished with Van Hale."

"Good idea."

Forty-five minutes later, the two Lennox detectives returned to their desks.

"OK. That's done. All processed and locked up. His lawyer is on his way here now. You two may want to make yourselves scarce before he gets here. He won't be happy to learn that you were involved in this without calling him up front."

"Good thinking. We're out of here," said Joe. "When do you expect the bail hearing?"

"Should be tomorrow morning."

"Court starts at ten," said Joe. "This'll come up sometime between ten and noon."

"Well done, guys," said Ginny. "We'll see you in court in the morning."

"Have a good evening."

"Same to you."

Despite it being rush hour, Joe and Ginny were back in Jasper Creek in about thirty minutes. A quick stop at the supermarket, and they were soon cooking dinner at Joe's house. Joe and Ginny discussed the case and their progress on it for close to an hour, after which they did a little TV watching. Then, off to bed.

CHAPTER 22

Joe and Ginny were sitting in the next-to-last row of seats in the county courthouse around the corner from their station by 9:40 the next morning. Fernald and Rodriguez arrived about ten minutes later. The detectives nodded to each other, and Fernald and Rodriguez sat close to the front. Two sheriff deputies had driven Van Hale from Lennox earlier that morning, and he was being kept in a holding cell on the courthouse's lower level.

It was close to eleven when Van Hale's bail hearing began. A sheriff's deputy escorted Van Hale and Ashley, his attorney, into the courtroom from a door near the front of the room. They sat at one table while two assistant prosecutors entered the courtroom and sat at another table, both groups facing the judge.

The hearing was over twenty minutes later. The assistant prosecutor made a fine presentation arguing for no release, outlining the heinous nature of the crime, the obvious attempt to cover up the crime's location and the killer's intent to frame a third party for the murder. Also emphasized was the relative wealth of the suspect, and the ease with which he could flee. The defense attorney was equally eloquent in recommending that Van Hale be released on his own recognizance, emphasizing that the charges had not yet been proven, that Van Hale had no criminal record, that Van Hale was a pillar of his community, owner and president of a large local company that employed many, and a happily married husband and father of two teenage boys.

Almost immediately after both sides made their cases, the judge ruled that bail be set at $2,500,000. He also ruled that Van Hale would surrender his passport to the court in the event of his release.

"I would have preferred he stay locked up, but the judge actually came to a reasonable decision," Joe whispered to Ginny.

"I agree. I'm amazed at how quickly he was able to come up with his decision."

"Probably a result of his having held a zillion hearings like this. Hell, he's probably thought about it and mostly made up his mind before the hearing even began."

"Yeah. I think you're right, Joe."

The two Lennox detectives walked over to Joe and Ginny.

"Well, that was short and sweet," said Rodriguez.

"Yes, it was," said Joe. "Like it almost always is. What say we grab a cup of coffee and figure out our next moves?"

"Good idea."

"Let's go down the street. The coffee's pretty good there," suggested Ginny.

"Works for us," said Rodriguez.

Ten minutes later, the four detectives were huddled over their coffee cups in an almost-empty Starbucks.

"Well, he'll be out in an hour or two. Someone like him won't have any problem raising the bail."

"Agreed," said Ginny. "Let's figure out our game plan

between now and the trial. With what we have so far, a guilty decision is far from a foregone conclusion."

"I want to make sure we keep showing progress. I really don't want your chief to have any reason to push us off the case."

"Not to worry, Joe," said Fernald. "Our chief is super pleased with the progress we've made regarding Van Hale."

"He should be," said Joe. "But I'm worried we might wind up unable to keep sending him progress reports at a fast enough clip."

"Joe, I share your concern," said Ginny. "But all we can do is just keep doing our best."

"OK, I get it," said Joe. "Ginny and I can start by doing a deep dive into the life and times of Van Hale. See what we can learn about his lifestyle, his marriage, previous affairs and so on."

"Sounds good," said Fernald. "And we'll head back to the apartment and that restaurant they frequented. See if we can find any more witnesses, learn anything new."

"All right, we've got our next steps. I also think that Joe and I need to go back to his company and interview or re-interview some of the executives. Someone may have seen or heard something dealing with Van Hale and the vic."

"Good idea. We're outta here now, heading back to Lennox. Let's stay in touch over the next few days."

"Will do," said Joe. "Probably by early next week the four of us should sit down with the prosecutor who'll be handling this and go over what we have and don't have."

"Right. And thanks for the coffee."

"Our pleasure," said Ginny.

Joe and Ginny were back at their desks a few minutes later. They decided that Ginny would dig into Van Hale while Joe focused on his company. Not wanting to break for lunch, Joe and Ginny accepted Jones and Caruso's offer to bring lunch back for them from the Chinese restaurant they were going to. Joe and Ginny barely stopped working while they had their wonton soup, egg rolls and lo mein. With rice, of course.

At about 2:30, Joe said, "OK, that's it. I'm brain-dead. I now know more about the pipe industry and National Pipe than I ever thought I would. Or ever wanted to. Ginny, let's share what we've learned. I need a change of pace. You go first, I want to hear about something other than pipe."

"Oh, you poor thing. I feel so, so sorry for you," said Ginny, with a big smile.

"You can't fool me. I'm a detective. I can tell you're being sarcastic."

"Right you are. OK, here's what I learned so far. He's 49 years old. His father was president and owner of National Pipe and his mother was a stay-at-home mom, after being a nurse before they had children. He went to the University of Toledo, and graduated with a degree in mechanical engineering. Right out of school he went to work for National Pipe, becoming president 15 years ago when his father retired. He became owner after his father died nine years ago."

"Anything on the personal side?"

"Hold on. I was just getting to that. He married his wife, a Barbara Gibbons, about five years before he became president. They have two teenage boys, 16 and 18, and he seems to have been a model citizen: Rotary Club, Chamber of Commerce, even on the board of the local United Way."

"Anything about past crimes? Trouble at home? That kind of thing."

"A couple of speeding tickets is all I could find. There may or may not have been problems at home, but it never reached the point of a legal or police matter."

"Not surprising. We'll probably only learn those juicy details by talking with friends and neighbors."

"Sounds like that's one of our next steps. What did you learn about the company?"

"Interesting history. It was started by his grandfather. He immigrated to the US from Holland. Spent a few years in New York City, then moved to Columbus as a salesman for a pipe manufacturer in New Jersey. After a few years he quit that job and opened up a distributor business, handling pipe and related products, like connectors and faucets, here in Jasper Creek. Another few years, he started doing some limited manufacturing work. Gradually the distributor part of the business got smaller as the manufacturing part got larger."

"The great American success story. I love it."

"I agree. Anyhow, when the grandfather retired, Van Hale's father took over. Then, as you also found out, Van Hale replaced him when he retired, and then inherited the business when his father died."

"Anything else?"

"Two things that might prove useful to us."

"Go for it. I'm listening."

"Turns out that Van Hale doesn't quite own one hundred percent of the company. Three families, descendants of friends of the grandfather, owned a combined 20% of the total."

"And?"

"Over the years, Van Hale bought out two of the three families. We might want to talk with them, or at least with the remaining shareholder. Although Van Hale, with his current 90% ownership, can make all the decisions, he legally has to do so in a way that doesn't screw the minority shareholder. Fiduciary responsibility and all that mumbo jumbo."

"Yeah, it would be interesting to see if they feel like they've been treated fairly by Van Hale."

"My thoughts, exactly."

"And the second thing?"

"Turns out that for the most recent plant expansion, about four years ago, the company borrowed several million from two banks."

"So? That doesn't sound too unusual to me."

"No, it's not. The unusual part is the investigation currently underway, launched by the two banks."

"Oh?"

"Seems that in reviewing the financial results, the banks concluded that a fair amount of money seemed to be disappearing. They've had a forensic accounting group working at the company for the past few months, trying to sort things out."

"You mean, like someone might be skimming somehow? That's definitely worth learning more about. Hell, it might even be the motive for Knox's killing. As

CFO, she probably was either involved in it or found out about it."

"We made some good progress this afternoon. Let's have dinner out to celebrate."

"Works for me, Joe. But let's be clear: we're celebrating our progress, not success. We've still got a ways to go for that."

"Full agreement. What are you in the mood for — steak or barbecue?"

"You know I love 'em both. But celebration calls for steak, not barbecue."

"OK. Let's go with Johnny's Chophouse. I'm sure we don't need a reservation. It's Thursday. But what say we go try to talk with some of Van Hale's neighbors first?"

"Works for me."

Ginny and Joe spent about 90 minutes in Van Hale's neighborhood. Ringing a dozen doorbells resulted in seven discussions. Everyone spoke highly of Van Hale. A successful businessman, involved in several local civic and charitable organizations. A good family man. Unfortunately, his work kept him away from home many evenings and part of most weekends, but that wasn't surprising for someone running a company as large as National Pipe.

Joe and Ginny were disappointed, but not surprised. They already knew of Van Hale's civic and charitable activities, and working late was both an expected responsibility of a senior executive and a great cover for one or more affairs.

Joe was right about the restaurant. They were seated immediately and had a relaxing and enjoyable meal.

Between bites, they talked through all they had to do starting the next morning. Despite satisfaction with the progress-to-date, Joe repeated his nagging fear of the Lennox police chief pulling the case away from Joe and Ginny.

CHAPTER 23

By 8:30 the next morning, Joe and Ginny were in the conference room, using the speaker phone to talk with Fernald and Rodriguez, who were similarly on a speaker phone in Lennox.

"Good going, guys," said Fernald. "Sounds like you dug up some information about financial shenanigans definitely worth pursuing. I wish I could say we were as successful. We talked to a lot of people at the apartment complex. Several knew about a couple in that apartment, and a few recognized one or both of their photos, but we really didn't learn anything we don't already know. We plan to do the same thing at the restaurant today, but our hopes for a breakthrough aren't too high. Anything we can help you guys follow up on?"

"Definitely," said Joe. "How about you interview the three minority shareholders, while Ginny and I deal with the two banks and their forensic audit?"

"Works for us," said Rodriguez. "Send us the names and contact info and we'll get right on it."

"Great. We'll fax it as soon as we hang up. Oh, and have a nice weekend if we don't speak again today," said Ginny.

"Thanks. Same to you two."

After hanging up and faxing the information to the Lennox detectives, Joe and Ginny spent about ten minutes with the chief, bringing him up to date on what they'd learned and telling him what they and the Lennox detectives were planning to do next.

"Sounds good. Thanks for the update. Seems like you're actually starting to make some progress. Finally. Well done."

Back at their desks, Ginny said, "Once again, it's hard to tell if we just got a compliment or a kick in the butt. He has a magical way of doing that."

"You're right. If I had to bet, we probably got both."

"OK. Should we make appointments at those two banks?"

"Yup. Here're the banks, and the names of the person at each bank dealing with National Pipe. Let me see if I can get appointments with both of them for later today."

While Joe was making these calls, Ginny's phone rang.

"Morning, Ginny."

"Hi, Sarge. What can I do for you?"

"Someone here to see you and Joe. Want me to send him up, or do you want to come down and get him?"

"Depends. Who is it?"

"A Philip Van Hale."

"Huh? That's surprising. He just got out on bail yesterday. Wonder why he's here?"

"Didn't say."

"OK. I'm on my way down to get him."

As Joe was still on the phone, Ginny just gave Joe a quick wave and headed downstairs. Ginny looked around, but didn't see Van Hale. She walked up to the desk sergeant.

"Where is he, Sarge? I don't see him. Taking a pee break?"

"He's over there, sitting on the bench."

Ginny looked over and saw a teenage boy sitting nervously on the bench. Confused, she walked over and introduced herself.

"Hi. I'm Philip Van Hale. I need to talk to you."

"Philip Van Hale?"

"Well, officially, it's Philip Van Hale, Jr. You're the one who arrested my father. And you made a big mistake."

"Mr. Van Hale, actually it was the Lennox Police Department who arrested him. But let's go upstairs so we can talk."

Ginny led him upstairs and left him in the conference room while she went to get Joe.

"Joe, Van Hale's son is here. In the conference room. Says we made a big mistake arresting his father."

Joe followed Ginny into the conference room, introduced himself and sat down across the table from Van Hale.

"Mr. Van Hale, what's this about? Why did you say arresting your father was a big mistake?"

"Because he didn't do it."

"I'm not surprised that his son would feel that way. But tell us, how do you know that?" asked Joe.

"Because it was me that killed Kathryn."

"What? Say that again," said Ginny.

"You heard me. I killed Kathryn Knox. So, my father couldn't have. You arrested an innocent man."

"Before we go any further, Mr. Van Hale, how old are you? If you're a minor, we really need one of your parents to consent to these discussions. And they'd have the right to sit in with you."

"That's not an issue. I turned 18 four months ago."

"OK, then. You're an adult. At least for this purpose. Does anyone know you're here?"

"No."

"Let me get my tape recorder so that we have a clear record of what's said. This can be beneficial to you as well as us. Then, I want to read you your rights."

"OK."

And Joe did just that. He went back to his desk and returned with his tape recorder. He recorded the initial who, what and where, had Van Hale confirm his age, and then read Van Hale his Miranda rights.

"Yes, I understand all that. And I don't want a lawyer."

"Are you sure?" asked Ginny.

"Yes."

"OK, then. But you can change your mind at any time and ask for a lawyer."

"I understand."

"Mr. Van Hale, please repeat, now that the recorder is on, how you know that your father didn't kill Ms. Knox."

"Because I did. It was an accident, but I did it."

"Please walk us through it," said Ginny.

"OK. Turns out that my father has been cheating on my mother for years. I don't know how many years, or how many women, but a lot. And it was gradually killing my mother. At first she put up a good front, making believe that nothing was going on. But you could see what it was doing to her. Usually, she never knew who the women were. But this time, she somehow learned, or figured out, that it was Kathryn."

"Do you know how she found out?" asked Joe.

"No."

"Mr. Van Hale," said Ginny, "you refer to Ms. Knox as Kathryn. Did you know her?"

"Yeah. Pretty well. Every summer my brother and I worked at National Pipe. Our father was grooming us to someday take over. We'd rotate through most of the departments of the company — he wanted us to know all about the infrastructure. Part of each summer we worked in the Finance Department. Plus, Kathryn, and her husband before they got divorced, used to come to various company parties and dinners that would sometimes include us. So, my brother and I got to know her fairly well."

"Was your brother also involved with her murder?"

"What? No! Not at all. It was just me."

"OK. Please tell us exactly what happened."

"Like I said, my mother knew that my father was cheating on her again. She also somehow learned that it was with Kathryn. My brother and I heard enough of my parents arguing and my mother crying to know my father was having an affair, but we didn't know with who."

"OK," said Ginny. "So what happened the night of Ms. Knox's murder?"

"My brother was out with some friends. My mother got a call from my father, and she started crying hysterically after she hung up. I went and asked her what was wrong. She said it was nothing. That she was just sad my father had to work late that night. Well, I'm not dumb. First off, my father often had to work late, but this was the first time that my mother became hysterical over it. Secondly, this was Friday evening. Pretty doubtful that any work had to get done that night. Especially since my father often worked much or all of most weekends. So, I decided to check."

"What? How? What did you do?"

"I drove to my father's office and parked down the street, from where I'd be able to see him when he drove out of the lot."

"And?"

"Sure enough. He drove out about a quarter to seven. I carefully followed him, trying to be sure one or two cars stayed between us so he wouldn't see me."

"Then what happened?"

"He drove all the way to Lennox and parked in a shopping center parking lot. I parked at one end of the lot and got out of my car. I was careful not to let him see me as I followed him. Then, I was surprised to see him meet up with Kathryn. I was even more surprised by how they kissed each other hello. Then they walked into some Italian restaurant. By then, I was more than suspicious. I mean, he often had dinners with Kathryn or another of his executives. But why all the way in Lennox? And why on a Friday night? And that wasn't just a friendly little kiss on the cheek."

"What happened next?"

"I stayed in the parking lot until they came out, almost an hour and a half later. Man, I was frozen stiff. It was wicked cold out. I had a warm jacket, along with my hat and gloves, but the cold just came right through to me. Finally, they came out of the restaurant and went to my father's car. I was thrilled just to be able to go back to my car and turn the damn heat on. I then followed them for a few minutes to some garden apartment complex."

"What did you do then?" asked Ginny.

"Despite still being frozen, I got out of my car and followed them to see where they were heading. Kathryn was the one with the key. She opened apartment C-217 — I'll never forget that number — and they both went in. I think C was the building and 217 was the actual apartment number."

"Did you go into the apartment?" asked Ginny.

"Not right way. I went back to my car and sat there with the heat blasting. I was still frozen. More importantly, I was shocked and pissed at what I'd seen. Mostly at my father, but also at Kathryn. She knew he was married. Hell, she'd had dinners at our house that my mother had cooked and served her. I sat there, getting madder and madder, but not knowing what to do."

"For how long?"

"I don't really know. Maybe 15 minutes. Maybe 30. I was like in a daze and lost track of everything, including the time. Then, all of a sudden, I decided enough was enough. I decided it was time to confront the two of them and somehow make them stop seeing each other, or to be more accurate, screwing each other."

"So, what did you do?"

"I went to the apartment and rang the bell. I had to ring it three times, but Kathryn finally opened the door. I'll never forget the look of shock and fear on her face when she saw me. That was worth a million bucks to me."

"What did she do?" asked Ginny.

"She mumbled and fumbled for a minute, but then let me in and led me upstairs. It was a funny layout. There was a little foyer right inside the door, but you had to go up a flight of steps to actually get into the rest of the apartment. When I got upstairs, my father was standing in the living room. He looked as shocked and fearful as Kathryn did. But he also looked mad."

"What happened next?"

"My father started talking, but I wasn't listening. I started yelling at both of them, trying to lecture them on what they were doing, what it was doing to my mother and our family, and how they had to stop."

"And what were their reactions?" asked Joe.

"No idea. I was so enraged I never noticed."

"What happened next?"

"Somehow, at one point I was standing directly in front of Kathryn. I leaned forward so my face was only inches from hers, and I started calling her all kinds of names, threatening to tell everyone about their affair. Who knows what else I said? As I yelled louder and kept getting more and more in her face, she started to back up. Then, all of a sudden, she was in front of the stairs and started to fall. I tried grabbing her, but before I could get a good grip on her arm, she was gone. Flying down the stairs. I'll never forget the sound when she hit the floor at the bottom of the steps, right in front of the door I had entered only a few minutes earlier."

"Are you sure you didn't push her?" asked Joe.

"Definitely. I swear. I wanted them to end their affair. I didn't want her, or anyone, to die."

"Then what happened?"

"I raced downstairs, took off one of my gloves and checked her pulse. She was clearly dead. I'm not a doctor, but from her position on the floor I was pretty sure she had a broken neck."

"And your father?"

"He slowly came down the stairs. When I said she was dead, he just nodded. He was, like, in shock. I'd never seen him paralyzed like that before. Usually, he's a man of action who can handle anything."

"What happened next?" asked Joe.

"I took off my other glove and pulled out my phone to call 9-1-1. But my father stopped me. He said to hold on for a minute while we figured things out.

"So I put my phone away. A few minutes later, my father had a plan. He went back upstairs and brought down a bedspread. We rolled Kathryn's body in it. He opened the garage door, then went and got his car and parked it in the garage and closed the door. He had me help him carry her and put her into his trunk. I didn't know what he was going to do, but he said it was better if I didn't know. He told me to go back to Jasper Creek, find some of my friends and hang out with them. This would help establish an alibi for me. He emphasized that we could never tell anyone about this. Never. He then put his hat and coat on, took Kathryn's pocketbook and locked the apartment door as we left. He threw her pocketbook into the trunk and closed it. He got into his car and drove off. I closed the garage door, went to my car and headed to Jasper Creek. Like he had said, I hooked up with some buddies and we hung out for a few hours. And that's it."

"Mr. Van Hale," said Ginny, "why are you telling us this now?"

"Because my father's trying to take the fall for me. That's

not right. His affair and stuff was terrible, but it wasn't murder. And Kathryn's death really was an accident, and I'm thinking that you might believe it more if you knew it was me and not him."

"Well, thank you for coming forward. I'm afraid we're going to have to keep you here, at least for today, until we sort things out with the prosecutor."

"I understand."

"We'd also like to take your fingerprints. They may help corroborate your story."

"OK, you can. But it won't help. I had my gloves on almost the whole time, so I doubt if there are any of my fingerprints in that apartment."

"Understood," said Joe. "But let's get them. Just in case. Mr. Van Hale, would you be willing to take a polygraph test?"

"You mean a lie detector?"

"Yes, that's what it's often called. It would help to confirm your credibility."

"Sorry, but no. I've read too many articles about getting false results because the person is nervous, and stuff like that. This is too important to risk something like that happening."

"Too bad, but that's your legal right to decide. One more thing," said Ginny. "It would help if you allowed us to check all your shoes for blood residue. That will help us conclude whether or not we believe you. You can sign a release, or we can get a warrant. Your call whether we go the easy or hard route."

"Happy to sign the release, but you won't find any blood. I was very careful to step around any blood on the floor."

He gave Ginny the key to his apartment. She walked downstairs, gave the key and the release form to the Crime Scene Department and asked them to check all shoes found in his apartment. Ginny checked the shoes he was wearing, but found them to be blood-free. After having Van Hale fingerprinted, Joe and Ginny locked him in one of the interrogation rooms and then returned to their desks.

"Yikes. Quite a development," said Ginny.

"When it rains, it pours. I don't know where we go with this, what with Van Hale, Sr. *and* Van Hale, Jr. Which one of them is really guilty? Or did they both do it? And was it really an accident?"

"Good questions, Joe. Too bad they're all without answers. I think we need to bring the chief up to date, and then we have to meet with Porter."

"Agreed. And for that, we need to invite Fernald and Rodriguez from Lennox."

"Definitely. OK, I'll go talk with the chief. Why don't you try to schedule the big powwow for sometime later today?"

"Will do."

A few minutes later, Ginny returned. "Joe, the chief appreciated the update, commenting that two updates in one day was an almost once-in-a-lifetime occurrence with us. And he definitely wants to attend the meeting later today."

"OK. And I got it set up. But the earliest we can do it is 3:30. Porter will be in court all afternoon until then."

"Shouldn't be a problem. A few hours in the room can't hurt Van Hale, Jr. that much. I'll arrange for him to get something to eat, and some water. I'll also tell the chief the time of the meeting."

"Sounds good. Then it's time for us to head for Sancho's. I'm starving."

"When aren't you?"

"Oh, shit. I have to call one of those two banks back. I scheduled a meeting with them for this afternoon. I'll try to reschedule it for Monday, so we'll have both our bank meetings on Monday."

CHAPTER 24

Joe and Ginny were back at their desks by one o'clock. A few minutes after they returned, Ginny got another call from the desk sergeant.

"Hi, Sarge. Can't live without me, can you?"

"Probably not, but that's not why I'm calling. You're getting more and more popular."

"Oh. How?"

"You've got another visitor. And from the same family. An Elliott Van Hale this time."

"What's going on? I'll be right down to get him."

Ginny brought this Van Hale to the conference room and left him there while she went to get Joe.

"Joe, you're not going to believe this."

"That's true of most things. Wanna be more specific?"

"Sure. Elliott Van Hale, Van Hale's younger son, is here to see us. I parked him in the conference room."

"Jeez. It's getting busy around here. I guess it stopped snowing and turned into a 'Van Halestorm.'"

"Ugh. Joe, that one's pretty bad. Even for you."

"Can't blame a guy for trying. Anyhow, let's go talk to him."

But the talking stopped right after it had begun. As he was only sixteen years old, Joe and Ginny couldn't talk with him without one of his parents being present, or at least giving written permission for the interview.

Van Hale called his mother. She was surprised and

upset, but agreed to come to the station right away. Joe and Ginny left him in the conference room and returned to their desks while waiting for Mrs. Van Hale.

"Joe, we should call the Lennox guys. They have to be here later for our big meeting. They might want to come early and watch or participate in this."

"Good idea. Go ahead and call them. While you're doing that, I'll go give the chief update number three for the day."

Ginny called Fernald and Rodriguez. The detectives thanked her and said they were on their way. The chief also told Joe to alert him when the interview began, as he'd like to observe it.

Less than an hour later, the second small interrogation room was crowded with Elliott Van Hale and his mother, Howard Ashley (their attorney), Ginny, and the two Lennox detectives. Joe and Ginny had agreed to let the Lennox detectives conduct this interview.

Joe and the chief stood outside, watching through the one-way observation window.

Ginny turned on her recorder, made all the introductions and recorded all the required initial information, including Van Hale's age, Ms. Van Hale's approval and the reading of Van Hale's Miranda rights.

At their lawyer's suggestion, Ms. Van Hale tried to rescind her approval. But her son got so upset and argued so vehemently that she agreed to let the interrogation proceed. She sat quietly as her son answered all the questions, totally ignoring their lawyer's repeated advice to remain silent.

Joe and Ginny were shocked. Van Hale's telling of what

occurred the night of Knox's murder was identical to that told by his older brother. Except for one item. This Van Hale said it was he and not his brother who followed their father, entered the apartment, yelled at Knox, tried to stop her from falling down the stairs and then helped his father get the body into his trunk, after which the younger Van Hale went to hang out with some of his friends in Jasper Creek.

Neither Joe nor Ginny was surprised when Ashley refused to allow them to take the younger son's fingerprints or test his shoes without a warrant, let alone have him undergo a polygraph exam.

As it was getting close to three o'clock, the four detectives and the chief walked over to the county prosecutor's office, leaving the younger Van Hale, along with his mother and their attorney, in the interrogation room. After about 15 minutes, Porter returned from court and led them all into a large conference room next door to his office.

"Good afternoon, everyone." After Porter and Fernald said hello to each other and Porter and Rodriguez were introduced to each other, Porter asked, "To what do I owe the pleasure of this esteemed gathering?"

"Charles, we've got a weird situation," said Joe.

"Oh, great. Weird is just what I need on a Friday afternoon. What's going on?"

Joe and Ginny spent about fifteen minutes summarizing the entire Knox murder case from the beginning: who their suspects had been, how Van Hale had been arrested, their digging into National Pipe and the plan for the Lennox detectives to meet with the one remaining and two former minority shareholders while Joe and Ginny met with the two banks on Monday.

"Sounds good to me. So what's the problem? And what's so weird?"

"We've got too many perps," said Ginny.

"Huh?"

Ginny summarized the evidence against Van Hale, his arrest and bail. She then described the surprising separate confessions of each of the sons. "So, any one of the three could be the perp, as could any two, or even all three. And was it really an accident? And who, and how many, were involved in moving the body? Is there a conspiracy and, if so, is it between just two of them, or all three? And if just two, which two?"

"Well, you were right about one thing," said Porter.

"What's that?" asked Joe.

"This is, indeed, a weird situation."

"So what do we do?" asked Ginny.

"That's easy," said Porter. "Figure out which one — or ones — did it, and then get enough proof for a conviction. Or even better, one, and only one, solid confession."

"We realize all that," said Joe. "But what do we do *now*?"

"Also easy. You need to release the two sons. With multiple-but-conflicting confessions, we don't have enough to hold them, much less charge them. Meanwhile, over the next couple of days I need to decide what to do about the father. We may have to drop all the charges against him for the same reason. Except perhaps for obstruction. Even the kids say that he's the one that drove the body away from the crime scene. But give me a couple of days to research this more fully."

"But, Charles, Van Hale, Sr.'s fingerprints are all over the apartment," said Ginny.

"And what about prints from the two kids?"

"Nada. Both described how they were wearing gloves most of the time they claim they were in the apartment," said Ginny. "And the lawyer won't let us take the younger son's prints without a warrant."

"So the lack of their fingerprints doesn't disprove their stories," said Porter. "Also, how did both boys know the layout of the victim's apartment and how she died falling down that flight of stairs if they weren't there? Unless their father told them all the details."

"You can thank my favorite reporters and cameramen," said Joe.

"How's that?" asked Porter.

"Once again," said Joe, "they make our job harder, and maybe even screw up the whole case. How she died, falling down the steps and all, has been on the news. Damn if I know where they get their info from. Someone in the PD, your office, the Crime Scene group or the medical examiner's office has a big mouth. And, thanks to a so-called helpful neighbor, one of the TV reporters and cameramen visited her one-bedroom, identically laid-out apartment. TV and the newspapers did it once again. I fully understand and believe in our Bill of Rights, but when it interferes with a murder investigation . . . ."

"I understood," said Porter. "But it is what it is."

"Jeez," said Joe. "Who would have thought we'd wind up with too many number-one suspects *and* too many confessions?"

"Yup," said Porter. "Sadly, more than enough to plant

serious reasonable doubt in the jurors' minds. OK. For now, release the two sons. I'll get us all back together early next week once I figure out what to do about Van Hale, Sr. And, in the meantime, finding some clear evidence of which one or two Van Hales is the real perp wouldn't hurt."

"Understood," said Ginny as all the others nodded.

The meeting then broke up, and everyone went their own way.

Back at their desks, Ginny had a message from the Crime Scene unit. They had checked all the shoes in Van Hale, Jr.'s apartment, but none of them had any blood on them.

Joe and Ginny released the two sons, telling them to check in before they left the state. They then spent about 30 minutes more at their desks, after which they headed to Joe's house for the weekend.

Over the weekend, Joe and Ginny's conversations centered on two topics. The first, of course, was the case. Despite trying to figure out how to determine, and then prove, which of the Van Hale's stories was the real one, they had no plan of action that they felt confident would get them to that objective. Ginny had to repeatedly reassure Joe that the Lennox chief was very unlikely to take over the case, given its current status. She even tried joking, "Joe, talk about progress. Look at how quickly we got to three confessed perps, not just one." But it did little to alleviate Joe's fear that having the case taken away would represent a performance blemish on his and Ginny's records.

The second topic of discussion was more personal.

"Ginny, this is crazy."

"What specific craziness are you referring to?"

"Do you realize we've spent almost every night here for at least the past six weeks?"

"And? Is that a problem?"

"No. The problem is that you're still paying for your condo, and it's serving as nothing more than a storage unit for some of your stuff."

"Yeah. I've been thinking about that. We're just throwing money away. You're right, it is crazy."

"Ginny, you ought to put it up for sale. No idea how long it will take to sell it. But when it does sell, we'll move your stuff here. Or, if we're that far along, to our yet-to-be-found-and-purchased new house."

"You're right, Joe. Let's look up a couple of realtors. We can then meet with each of them. Once we select one, they can get the process underway. I have no idea what my place could sell for, but the agents'll give us data about recent sales of similar condos and their estimate of what mine could be worth."

"Sounds like a plan."

Joe and Ginny spent a few hours researching local real estate firms and agents, and selected three that they'd plan to meet with.

CHAPTER 25

Monday morning, Joe and Ginny were on their way to Indianapolis to meet with a vice president at First Commerce Bank of Indianapolis, one of the two banks which had lent money to National Pipe.

At about eight o'clock, Ginny received a call on her cell phone from the medical examiner.

"Good morning, Doc. You're up early today. How can I help you?"

"Hi, Ginny. I'm actually calling to help you. We finished the autopsy on that Knox woman, and I figured you'd appreciate a quick summary."

"Most definitely. Hold on a sec. Joe's here in the car with me. Let me put you on speaker."

Joe and the medical examiner greeted each other, and then the ME started right in.

"We finished the autopsy last night. COD is definitely her broken neck. After reviewing things with Forensics and Crime Scene, it clearly resulted from her falling down that flight of stairs in the Lennox apartment. But we can't tell whether she was pushed or fell accidentally. There were no bruises on her body that couldn't be explained by her fall down the stairs, and there was no evidence of a struggle."

"So where does that leave us?" asked Ginny.

"No choice but for us to label the manner of death

'undetermined.' Sorry. I'm sure you guys aren't happy with the inconclusive conclusion. But it is what it is."

"We understand, Doc. When can we get your written report?"

"It'll be on your desk within 48 hours, Ginny."

"Super. Thanks, Doc."

"Don't mention it. Have a good day."

Joe and Ginny were discussing the call with the ME, when Ginny was called on her car radio. It was Dispatch, informing her that the chief wanted Joe and her to cancel their bank meeting and return to Jasper Creek as quickly as possible.

"Why? What's going on, Elaine?" asked Ginny.

"No idea. That's all the chief said. Hey, I gotta run. We're in the middle of an apparent suicide on the north side. See you later."

Ginny put the radio back on the hook, made a U-turn at the next emergency-vehicle turnaround on I-70 and headed east, back to Jasper Creek. While en route, Joe called the bank's vice president. Joe explained that something had come up, forcing them to cancel the meeting, but that he'd call to reschedule as soon as he could.

As soon as they were back at the station, Joe and Ginny went to see the chief.

"What's up, Chief? Why'd you have us abort our little jaunt to Indianapolis?" asked Joe.

"Don't know what it all means, but they found Van Hale, Sr.'s body behind a vacant row of storefronts over on the north side. First impression is suicide."

"What? My God!" said Ginny.

"Damn!" said Joe as he looked first at the chief, then at Ginny.

"You two ought to hightail it over there and check it out."

"Will do, Chief," said Joe. Shaken, he and Ginny walked back to Ginny's car and headed north. Joe called Dispatch and got the address.

"Boy, this one keeps throwing new twists at us," said Joe.

"That's for sure. Wonder if there's a note or something."

"We'll find out soon enough."

Joe and Ginny pulled into the parking lot and walked over to the Buick Regal, which they knew was Van Hale's. Standing around were the medical examiner, the Crime Scene team, the Patrol officer who was first on the scene and Detectives Caruso and Klein, who were temporarily assigned the case in Joe and Ginny's absence. The scene had been appropriately taped off, and a few other Patrol officers were keeping the press and curiosity seekers outside of the taped off area.

"Hi, everyone," said Ginny. "Whadda we have?"

"Looks pretty straightforward," said Caruso. "The vic, who we identified from his driver's license as Philip Van Hale, was found here. Dead behind the steering wheel. We assume it's his company car. Papers in the glove compartment list National Pipe as the lessee.

"Looks pretty likely he killed himself by asphyxiation. Flexible hose from the exhaust in through the driver's side window. He even stuffed rags around it to prevent any fresh air from getting in. Car was still running when we got here. I turned the engine off. Looks like the carbon monoxide did its thing."

"Did he leave a note?"

"Sure did. Sitting folded, right on his lap."

Caruso put on a pair of disposable gloves and took an evidence envelope from the passenger seat of his car. "Here it is. Want me to read it?"

"Sure," said Ginny. "Easier than putting on our own gloves."

"My pleasure," said Caruso as he took the note from the evidence bag and unfolded it. "Here goes. 'To whom it may concern, first off I want to say how much I love my wife and two sons, and how sorry I am about the pain that this will cause them. But I'm sure it will be less than if I had remained alive. The shame of what I've done would stick to them forever. I am so sorry for my numerous infidelities. I don't know why I indulged in them, for I love my beautiful wife more than life itself.

'And my two boys, I couldn't be prouder of either of them. The fact that they both tried to take the blame for Kathryn's death illustrates their total selflessness. But the truth is that her death was all my doing. Neither of my boys was even there. And, although you may not ever believe me, her death was an accident. We were arguing, she was backing away from me and fell down the whole flight of steps. I tried to stop her, but I couldn't.

'And I know that I only made things worse by removing Kathryn's body. But at the time I wasn't thinking straight, and I panicked. After driving around for several hours with her body in my trunk, I decided to put the body in Rick LaCroix's garage. That idea just came to me in a flash. I hated the way he used to treat Kathryn, but that of course is no justification. When I got to his house in the middle of the night, I found his unlocked car in his driveway, so I opened his trunk and put her in there instead of in his garage.

'Again, my deepest love and sincerest apology to my wife and sons, and my apologies to Rick and, of course, Kathryn.

'Philip Van Hale'"

"Wow!" said Ginny. "That seems to say it all."

"Doc," said Joe, "anything to add?"

"Not really. We'll want to do a full autopsy, but it sure looks like suicide. Probably died four to six hours ago."

"OK, thanks, Doc."

"Joe, let's head back to the station."

"Yup."

Back at their desks, Joe and Ginny continued discussing this surprising turn of events.

"One question, Joe."

"What's that?"

"Was everything in that note true, or was Van Hale trying to cover for one or both of his kids?"

"Super question, Ginny. But I think we may never know the answer. Were the two kids, or just one of them, lying to protect their father, knowing that all they needed to do was develop a reasonable alternate theory for the jury? Or was the father lying to protect one or both of his sons? Or, did two or all three of them do it and then jointly develop the multiple-confession strategy?"

"Regardless, the father took the final step all by himself to try to totally clear his kids."

"Let's fill the chief in. Then I think we need to reconvene the whole group in Porter's conference room."

Ginny and Joe filled the chief in, and were pleasantly surprised that he seemed to be satisfied with the case as it stood.

"Let's just say it was the father and be done with it. Guilty or not, losing their father is punishment enough for the two boys."

"Works for us, Chief. Let's see if Porter and our Lennox friends are on board with that," said Ginny.

Everyone, including Caruso, Klein, the two Lennox detectives and the two police chiefs, were back in Porter's conference room just after noon. Porter had ordered in three large pizzas and sodas, so everyone was chewing and drinking while speaking and listening.

"One thing before we get started," said Ginny. "We told some of you already, but just to be sure I want to state that the ME confirmed Knox's death was from her broken neck, resulting from her fall down the flight of stairs in the Lennox apartment. But he had to label it as 'undetermined.' They couldn't determine if she was pushed or fell accidentally."

"Thanks, Ginny. OK, assuming the medical examiner doesn't find out anything new about Van Hale's death," said Porter, "I think we should take this at face value. Van Hale's note said he was responsible, and we should accept that. We'll never know for sure if it was him and him alone, nor whether it truly was an accident or if Ms. Knox's fall was 'helped along.' So, we should just let it go. Same for possible obstruction of justice and conspiracy charges against the two kids. Losing your father is probably punishment enough. Anyone feel differently?"

"I tend agree with you," said the chief. "But even if the results weren't admitted into court, we'd know a lot more if the boys had agreed to polygraph exams."

"True enough," said Porter. "But it's their legal right to say no."

"I'm well aware of that. Too bad."

"Just one thought," said Zanelli, the Lennox police chief. "Are we pretty sure that there's not a totally different explanation? I don't know. Like the wife did it. Or some bad dealings with the business. They'd borrowed from two banks. Did they also borrow from the Mafia? I've got no evidence that it's any of this. Just want to be sure we get everything on the table."

"Good questions, George," said the chief, "but we haven't seen anything to suggest something like that. Of course, we also haven't seen anything to disprove any of that."

"I just wanted us to at least consider these possibilities. Charles, I'm OK with what you proposed."

Everyone nodded their agreement.

"OK, then," said Porter. "We're on hold until we get Van Hale's autopsy report. Unless it tells us something new, sounds like most or all of us are ready to wrap this up."

"Yup," said Joe. "But to tie things up nicely, Ginny and I are still going to meet with the two banks that lent money to National Pipe, and I'd recommend that Will and Juan still talk with the former and current minority share-holders. Never know what might turn up."

"Will do," said Fernald.

"And," said Ginny, "we still haven't figured out whether it was Van Hale, or Knox, or both of them who rented that apartment in Lennox. But it may not matter, since they're both deceased."

"All right," said Porter, "let's stay in touch until we get these remaining pieces of info. And I agree with you, Ginny, there's little value at this point in trying to determine who rented the apartment. We know who was using it."

Everybody mumbled or nodded their agreement.

Back at their desks, Ginny returned a call to Sorensen.

"Not that you need it given all the fingerprint and footprint evidence, but the DNA we found in the apartment matches the sample you took from Van Hale, Sr. So now you can be super certain that he was in that apartment."

Ginny thanked Sorensen, and then filled him in about Van Hale's suicide.

Joe and Ginny spent the rest of the day bringing their notes and paperwork on the case up to date.

"Joe, going through my notes, we still have one item left open."

"Hmm. What is it? I can't think of anything."

"We were going to follow up with Van Hale's wife and his executive secretary about his alibi, if any, for the time of the murder."

"Oh, yeah. Once again shows the value of your taking thorough notes of everything."

CHAPTER 26

The next day, Joe and Ginny spent the morning driving to and from Indianapolis. They met with the lending vice president at the First Commerce Bank of Indianapolis, who was the relationship officer for the National Pipe account. Once the discussion got started, the vice president asked one of the bank's workout officers and one of its forensic accountants to join the meeting.

"Yes, we made a fairly large loan, $2.5 million in fact, to National Pipe about three years ago. At the same time, Columbus National Bank came into the deal for $1.3 million. As we had the larger loan, we became the lead bank."

"What does that actually mean?" asked Ginny.

"To simplify matters, we negotiated the loan agreement, which then, except for the dollar amount of the loan, was used by both banks. We also were responsible for monitoring the loan and the company's adherence to all the terms of the agreement. For this effort, we received a few extra tenths of a percent interest rate compared to Columbus National."

"And how has that loan worked out so far?" asked Joe.

"Just fine for the first two years or so. But then things turned south."

"Oh? In what way?" asked Ginny.

"Well, their sales were continuing to grow, and their

receivables and inventory stayed in line with the sales growth. But their expenses seemed to grow a lot faster than sales. And we couldn't figure out where or why. It seemed a little here and a little there, which in total added up to a fairly large drop in profits. Despite the steady sales growth."

"And what happened next?" asked Joe.

"Well, they quickly went into technical default of their loan. How much do you know about finance?"

"Not much. Other than a lot of money is better than a little money."

"Sounds like you know the most important thing. But let me give you a little mini-lecture, if you don't mind. I think it'll help you understand the situation."

"Sure. Go for it," said Joe.

"Every loan, of course, has a big, bulky legal document that both parties sign. There's a whole lot of legal mumbo jumbo, but here's what it boils down to. There's basically three areas. The first deals with the amount of the loan, interest payments and the repayment schedule. This outlines the monthly payment of interest and the repayment of principal. These are a function of the loan amount, the life of the loan and the interest rate, which can either be set as a fixed percentage or can be defined relative to another rate, such as six percentage points higher than the consumer price index."

"OK, that's pretty clear. What's the next part?"

"Part two deals with what happens in case of default. If the company defaults on the loan, and we'll discuss this in more detail next, this section states the consequences. Most loans are secured by some assets and the lender gets these assets if the company defaults on the loan. These assets can be the building and equipment of the company, or the stock of the company, and, as is usually the case when the company is privately owned, the financial assets and even the house of the company's owner. If the banks then sell these assets for more than what the company owes them, the extra money goes back to the company or its shareholders."

"Taking all or most of the assets can be tough, but I understand the need for it."

"OK, that takes us to the third key part of the loan document. What default is. There are two types. The first is actual default, where the company fails to make an interest payment or principal repayment on time. The company is often given a 30-to 60-day grace period to get their payments back on schedule, but if they don't they're in default."

"And the second type?" asked Ginny.

"That's a bit more complicated. First off, when the loan is initially being considered and negotiated the company provides a huge amount of data, like prior financial statements, names of the largest customers, leases the company owes money on, current lawsuits and much, much more. If it turns out that any material part of this data is wrong or intentionally misleading or left out, the lender can declare the company in technical default. Secondly, the loan document also contains several financial data points and ratios that the company must meet or beat in the future. If they fall below any of these specified measurements, and don't get it fixed within a grace period, the lender can declare technical default."

"So that's sort of like making a forecast and then having to meet it."

"Correct. But it's only for the explicitly identified items forecast in the loan document. And it's a forecast for the entire period of the loan. It usually includes a minimum quarterly sales level, a minimum profit as a percent of sales, ratios of assets to liabilities and so on. And that's basically it."

"That was helpful," said Ginny. "Thanks. Now, what specifically happened with National Pipe?"

"Those unexplained cost increases I mentioned earlier caused a technical default because their margin rate, that's profit divided by sales, fell below the minimum ratio in the loan documents. They also caused cash as a percent of total assets to fall too low. In both cases, the company couldn't fix the problem, or even explain the causes."

"So then what happened?" asked Joe.

"That's why these two folks are here. I'll let them each tell their part of the story. Alan is with our workout group, and Evelyn is with Forensic Accounting. Alan, why don't you start?"

"Happy to. Once a borrower goes into default, unless the bank deems it to be a small amount or an unimportant detail, the loan gets transferred from the Loan Department to our Workout Department. Our job is to get the bank's money back. We take off our gloves and get tough with the company. No more good-relationship concerns, which is a key responsibility of the Loan Department. We try to negotiate with the company and its owners, we threaten to and often actually do get the courts involved, and so on. We'll try to control how the company is managed, we'll have it focus on generating cash, even by selling some assets and using that money to pay off, or at least pay down, the defaulted loan. The loan documents give us this control in case of default. Particular to National Pipe's loan, they also clearly state that the two banks get repaid equally in proportion to the amounts of their loans, and that these bank loans get paid back before money owed to anyone else is repaid."

"Pretty brutal-sounding," said Joe.

"It can be when it has to be. In this case, we were able to negotiate an agreement with Mr. Van Hale. The agreement automatically transfers to Mrs. Van Hale, who became the majority owner once her husband died. This agreement allowed us to basically manage the company, and generate cash any way we could. It allowed us to try to sell the company, or parts of it. We would get enough of the proceeds to repay our loans, interest due and all the expenses we incurred. Any proceeds left after that would go to the shareholders."

"And where are you in this process now?" asked Joe.

"We hired a management consultant who we've used in the past. He and the team he brought in are running the company. They're also looking for a potential buyer for the company, but it's still pretty early to see how that might turn out."

"How long has this been going on?" asked Joe.

"Just about three months now."

"Was Kathryn Knox, the company's CFO, involved in or at least aware of all this?" asked Ginny.

"Of course. We kept the arrangement fairly quiet, but

Ms. Knox was aware of everything, and, in fact, heavily involved from the beginning. As CFO, she'd have to be."

"Thank you," said Ginny. "And how about your group, Evelyn?"

"I'm one of four accountants in our Forensic Accounting group. This is a specialty area of accounting, mixed in with some auditing and detective-like skills, that focuses on financial items being disputed, either in or out of court. It often, although not always, deals with illegal activities."

"And how does that relate to the National Pipe situation?" asked Ginny.

"We're trying to identify how and why and where costs seem to have mysteriously increased. It's those cost increases that wound up putting them in default."

"And what have you found?" asked Joe.

"Well, it's too early to be sure, or even to fully quantify things, but it appears that the company was receiving fake invoices from several bogus suppliers. These invoices were approved and paid, and the money trail sort of disappeared. For now."

"Any theories?"

"Don't hold me to it, but it seems that Mr. Van Hale was involved. And Ms. Knox was very probably also involved."

"How can you tell?" asked Ginny.

"Almost all of those phony invoices were approved by Mr. Van Hale. And enough money was involved that it would be very surprising if the CFO was totally unaware of at least some of these payments."

"How much are we talking about?" asked Joe.

"Our investigation is still underway, but it looks like it's in the range of $3 million to just under $5 million. It seems to have started on a fairly low level a couple of years ago, but then accelerated quite a bit about six months ago."

"Wow," said Joe. "We're talking real money here."

"Yes, we are."

"And what will you do about your findings?" asked Ginny.

"For now, we're continuing to research and investigate things. And we're trying to follow the money flows through a series of domestic and foreign shell companies. But my guess is that once the bank is fairly certain it'll recover all of its funds, probably through the company being sold, and with both Mr. Van Hale and Ms. Knox being deceased, we'll probably just stop investigating this and move on to other problem loans. After all, our job is to make the bank whole. It's not our job to try to ensure justice is achieved."

"Understood," said Joe. "Anything else?"

"Don't think so. Unless you have questions."

"No, I think we're good to go. Thank you very much for the time. And for the education. It was very enlightening."

"You're most welcome. Don't hesitate to call if you have other questions."

Joe and Ginny were soon in the car heading to Columbus National Bank with, of course, a stop for lunch along the way.

"That was a useful meeting, Joe. We learned a lot about

bank lending in general, as well as the details about National Pipe."

"Yeah, the banks are nice and friendly and helpful when things are going well, but can quickly turn cut-throat when they have to."

"You bet. Makes taking out a mortgage pretty scary."

"Can't disagree with that. But it's next to impossible to buy a house without a mortgage. Unless you're a million-aire, of course."

"Guess that means we'll be getting a mortgage when we get around to buying a house."

"'Fraid so."

"Speaking of which, we still have to contact those three realtors we wanted to meet with about selling my condo."

"For sure. And we really ought to do it sooner rather than later."

Joe and Ginny spent about 45 minutes with the Columbus National Bank vice president. It was basically the same story they had heard that morning in Indianap-olis, except there were fewer details about the default, workout and forensic accounting, since all of that was being handled by the Indianapolis bank on behalf of both banks.

While Joe was driving back to Jasper Creek, Ginny called Detectives Fernald and Rodriguez and put them on speaker for Joe's benefit. She summarized the bank meetings for them. In exchange, the Lennox detectives summarized their visits with the two former and the one remaining minority shareholder of National Pipe. None of the three had any complaints. They all felt that they were treated fairly. They received their dividend checks on time, and the two that had sold their shares felt that Van Hale had made them generous offers. All three described Van Hale as an honorable, trustworthy man, with two of the three using the term "pillar of the community."

CHAPTER 27

The next morning, Joe and Ginny drove to National Pipe to speak with Carol Nesbitt, who had been executive assistant to both Van Hale and Knox.

"Yes, Detectives. How can I help you?"

"Ms. Nesbitt," said Ginny, "first of all, we're very sorry for your loss."

"I can't believe it. First Kathryn, and now Mr. Van Hale. What is wrong with this world?"

"Ms. Nesbitt, one question. Could you please check Mr. Van Hale's agenda? We'd like to know if it shows any appointments around the time of Ms. Knox's death. That would be the evening of Friday the 24th, or early in the morning on Saturday the 25th."

"Hold on, let me bring it up on my screen."

Then, a minute later, "No, there's nothing showing. He had an early afternoon meeting that Friday. Then nothing until Monday."

"Did he often have meetings or go places without it being on his agenda?"

"Sure. I mean, major scheduled meetings and trips were almost always on it. But, Mr. Van Hale would often have last minute, ad hoc meetings or short trips that rarely made it onto the agenda. They were often over before I even knew about them."

"Makes sense," said Joe.

"And he rarely listed weekend informal meetings, or times he came to the office over the weekends. And, unless it was business related, anything that he and Mrs. Van Hale did over weekends was not put on his agenda. Mrs. Van Hale was quite good at keeping track of their private social life and making sure that Mr. Van Hale didn't miss any event."

"Could you also check that same time period on Ms. Knox's agenda?"

"Sure. Just give me a minute." Then, "Nothing after three on Friday, and nothing scheduled for that Saturday."

"Well that's all we needed to check. Thank you for your help."

"Do you know how Kathryn and Mr. Van Hale died? Did someone kill her? Do you know who? Did you confirm that Mr. Van Hale's death was, indeed, a suicide?"

"Ms. Nesbitt, that's what we're still working on. We think we're getting close to the answers, but it's an active investigation and we can't say anything."

"I understand."

"Again, thanks for your help, and our most sincere sympathies."

Joe and Ginny were soon back in Joe's car. While Joe was driving back to the station, Ginny called Ashley to schedule a meeting with his client, Mrs. Van Hale, to check what she knew about her husband's schedule around the time of Knox's death.

"Sorry, Detective, but that's not going to happen. Mrs. Van Hale largely blames you and your partner for her husband's suicide. Even if you could force her into an interrogation, you'd get nothing more than a bunch of

'I don't remembers.' And if those didn't work, there be the fifth amendment to fall back on. So I suggest you not waste everyone's time, including yours."

"Thank you, Mr. Ashley. And thank your client for all her cooperation. We'll be back in touch if and when we're ready to pursue this further."

"That would be my pleasure. Have a nice day."

After Ginny filled Joe in on Ashley's comments, Joe replied with, "Damn."

"I agree. But it is what it is. And if she really blames us, I can understand her reluctance."

"Yeah, but she could also be reluctant 'cause she doesn't want to confirm that Van Hale had no alibi."

"Correct, but we'll probably never know. One more example of the value of a good lawyer."

"Yup."

Joe parked in the PD parking lot, and he and Ginny walked over to Sancho's for lunch.

Back at their desks after lunch, Joe had a message to call the medical examiner.

"Hi, Doc. Joe McFarland. Got a message to call you back."

"Yes, hi, Joe. I've got the results of Van Hale's autopsy. Figured you'd want an oral rather than waiting for the official report."

"You bet. Let me put you on the speaker. Ginny's here with me."

"Hi, Doc."

"Hi, Ginny. Well, Guys, our conclusions are pretty straightforward. Plain old suicide. Asphyxiation. No signs of foul play, no needle marks or drugs in the system, no bruising or defensive marks. Nothing under his finger-nails. The written report will, of course, have a lot more of the usual blah-blah-blah, but that's the essence of it."

"Are you one hundred percent sure, Doc?"

"Hell no, Joe. We can never be one hundred percent sure when we're dealing with human beings, be they dead or alive. This is science, but it's not like math, where you can be one hundred percent sure that two plus two equals four. But I am as sure as I ever can be."

"That's good enough for us, Doc. Thanks a lot. Do me a favor, when you send out the written report, give me an extra copy. I want to share it with the folks in Lennox who worked on this case with us."

"Will do. Take care."

After hanging up, Joe said, "Looks like that's it then. Time to reconvene the big meeting in Porter's conference room."

"Yup."

Joe and Ginny shared the job of calling everyone, and the meeting was scheduled for 9:30 the next morning.

CHAPTER 28

The meeting in Porter's conference room didn't take long. Joe and Ginny informed everyone about the inconclusive meeting with Van Hale's executive assistant, the uncooperative position of Mrs. Van Hale's attorney and the medical examiner's findings surrounding Van Hale's death.

"OK then, that's it," said Porter. "We all agreed that, unless the autopsy pointed to something suspicious, we'd all accept that Van Hale's death was a suicide. And it resulted from his guilt or shame about his affair with Knox and her death. We'll never know whether her fall was truly an accident, or whether he helped her a bit.

"We'll get our press folks to get a statement out, and set up a press conference for later this afternoon. I'd like all four of you detectives and, if possible, both you chiefs to be there. As this is officially a Lennox PD case, you need to be there, George. You and at least one of your detectives should be prepared to say a few words. And I want to emphasize few — we want to keep this short and sweet."

With that, Porter stood up, said his good-byes and left the conference room to return to his office. The chiefs and detectives all thanked each other for their cooperation and stated how they'd enjoyed working together. They said their good-byes after confirming their intent to be at the press conference later that day.

Back at her desk, Ginny called Knox's parents in Massachusetts to inform them of the conclusion of the case and Van Hale's suicide. She spoke with Mr. Knox, with his wife at his side. They were surprised and somewhat relieved. "Detective, thank you so very much for calling us. It's a shock, of course, to learn that Katie was having an affair with her boss, but we're grateful that her murderer has been identified and so-called justice achieved, even though justice was administered by the murderer's own hand. His suicide, along with his moving Katie's body, convinces me that Katie's death was murder, not an accident."

Given that Knox's death was officially a Lennox case, Joe and Ginny then put copies of all their notes and paperwork in an envelope to give to Fernald and Rodriguez.

At three o'clock, Porter, the two chiefs, the four detectives and a group of reporters and cameramen were gathered in the hallway outside of the county prosecutor's office. Porter made the initial opening speech, congratulating the Lennox Police Department, ably assisted by the county Forensics group and the Jasper Creek Police Department and Crime Scene group, for solving this complicated case. After briefly describing the final conclusions surrounding the case, he introduced Chief Zanelli, who made similar remarks and then introduced Detective Fernald. Fernald merely thanked all who had assisted him and his partner in solving the case. He emphasized all the help from Joe and Ginny, reminding the media folks that this had been a Jasper Creek case until the apartment was discovered in Lennox and identified as the crime scene. When he mentioned Joe and

Ginny's names, they both smiled, gently nodded and raised their empty right hands as if they were offering a toast.

As the press conference ended and the session was breaking up, Joe and Ginny again thanked Fernald and Rodriguez, emphasizing what a pleasure it had been to work together, contrary to Joe's early expectations and the stereotyped antagonisms between departments. Ginny also gave the envelope with her and Joe's notes to Fernald.

The hallway was soon empty as everyone went their own way.

Back again at their desks, Ginny said, "Joe, there's one more important loose end we need to tie up."

"Oh? What's that?"

"We said we'd have a celebration dinner at La Pentola once the case was closed. Remember?"

"Yes, you're right. Your memory is better than most elephants."

"Thank you so much for the compliment."

"What say we invite Fernald and Rodriguez, along with their whatevers, to join us?"

"Great idea. I'll call them back right now."

CHAPTER 29

On Saturday evening almost two weeks later, Joe and Ginny entered La Pentola at about six-thirty. The manager immediately led them to a table for six in one corner of the restaurant. Fernald and his wife were already there. Introductions were made, and small talk ensued for about ten minutes, at which point Rodriguez and his girlfriend arrived.

Shortly thereafter, Rosa came over, gave everyone menus and took their order for two bottles of not-cheap Chianti from Joe. She, of course, recognized Joe and Ginny, and they spoke briefly about the case and its final outcome.

The six had an enjoyable dinner. Toward the end, Joe raised his glass and said, "I'd like to congratulate all of us for solving this case, even with the unusual twists at the end. More importantly, I have an apology to make to Will and Juan."

"Oh?" said Fernald as Rodriguez asked, "For what?"

"Based on a series of bad experiences I had being on all kinds of task forces in Chicago, I was really upset when our chief first told us we'd have to work with you, and that you two would be officially in charge. Ginny can confirm how pissed I was." Ginny nodded her head up and down with a big smile on her face.

"In her typical optimistic way, Ginny kept saying that it would be fine, that I should give you guys a chance.

Well, despite my poor expectations, Ginny was right. It was a pleasure working with you two, and none of my fears ever came to be. So, thank you. And here's to hoping we get to work together again."

Everyone toasted to that. Ginny was proud of Joe's willingness to bare his beliefs, admit that he had been wrong and actually thank Fernald and Rodriguez.

Joe picked up the bill, and everyone thanked him. After promising to stay in touch and getting together again soon, the party broke up and the couples each went their own way.

CHAPTER 30

Six weeks later, Ginny was drinking her coffee and watching the news while Joe was busy toasting two bagels. It was a pleasant Saturday morning, and Ginny was looking forward to a relaxed lazy day.

"Hey, Joe. Quick. Come here. You gotta see this."

Joe turned around and walked over to Ginny. He looked at the TV screen to which Ginny was pointing.

"Wha—"

"Shh. Listen to what she's saying."

". . . may recall the tragic death of the CFO, Kathryn Knox, and the resultant suicide of the president and owner, Philip Van Hale, of National Pipe here in Jasper Creek. Here with us today is Kenneth Albright, a management consultant brought in by the company's lenders to temporarily run the company. Good morning, Mr. Albright. Thanks for joining us."

"My pleasure to be here."

"Mr. Albright, as you know, there are many rumors swirling around about the sale of National Pipe. What can you tell us?"

"First of all, my and my team's primary and immediate priority has been to run the company. We're excited about the progress we've been making. Order backlog is up significantly, sales are starting to climb faster than before and profits are improving. A successful company is best for its employees as well as the entire community."

"That's great. But, what about the sale of the company? Are all those rumors correct?"

"I'm pleased to say that we've just recently signed a letter of intent for Consolidated Pipe and Tube in Houston to acquire us. As they are a public company, they're required to make this information public and are doing so right now."

"Can you give us some details?"

"Sure. A letter of intent is far from a done deal, but things look encouraging. We still have to negotiate a large number of details and develop the actual legal agreements, but I think a sale in four to six months is quite likely. Now before anyone panics, let me say a few other things. Although nothing is certain or forever in this day and age, if this deal goes through, Consolidated Pipe will be keeping this business operating here in Jasper Creek for the foreseeable future."

"How can you be so sure, Mr. Albright?"

"First off, our products offer an attractive diversification for Consolidated. Their products are used almost exclusively in the oil and gas industry. Ours are widely used in many different industries. Also, this will be their first business in the eastern part of the country and they're excited about the geographical expansion. They're even thinking of using part of our facilities as an eastern warehouse for their existing products. Plus, they realize that if they move the plant, not only will it be expensive to move or duplicate the manufacturing equipment, but they risk losing all the knowledge that's in our employees' heads. Despite trying to write down all the details of the manufacturing process, very few companies have successfully captured in writing all the little tricks of the trade and qualitative factors involved in manufacturing their products."

"Are they guaranteeing that they'll leave this business here?"

"No. And I don't think any company would. But Consolidated has good strategic and financial reasons to keep it here, and that's probably the most reassuring thing we could ask for. As I said earlier, I think this is exciting news for all our employees and for the city of Jasper Creek."

"Thank you for your time and comments this morning, Mr. Albright."

"My pleasure. Thank you for having me."

"After a short break, we'll be back with an exclusive interview with one of the Van Hale family members."

Joe and Ginny used the few minutes of commercials to grab their bagels, spread the cream cheese and start eating.

"We're back now. We have an exclusive interview with Philip Van Hale, Jr., the older son of Philip Van Hale, the owner and president of National Pipe until his recent death. We caught up with Philip Jr. here in Jasper Creek. He's finishing his senior year at Jasper Creek High. Good morning, Philip."

"Good morning."

"Before we get started, we also tried to contact your mother and younger brother, but we couldn't locate them. Any idea where they are?"

"Yes. My mom is taking an extended trip through

Europe. After all that's happened, she felt she needed a long break to get over it all."

"And your brother?"

"He's living someplace other than Ohio, but he'd not like me to say where. He's enjoying his anonymity . . . and will need some more time to fully process and accept everything that's happened.

"Although my family is no longer running National Pipe, I'm glad to hear that it's doing well and is likely to be sold to a company that will keep it here in Jasper Creek. That's great for all the wonderful employees and for the city. It should also be good for my mom. As you probably know, my father's death was a suicide. Most of his life insurance policies have a payout exclusion for suicides within the first two years of the policy. So, his few newer policies won't pay my mother anything, but his older policies will. And we hope she'll get something from the sale of the company after the banks get fully repaid. Also, she'll be selling our house after I'm off to college in the fall. With all that's gone on and how extensively it was covered by the media, I seriously doubt she'll want to continue living in Jasper Creek."

"And you, Philip?"

"I'm living in our house now. Then I'm off to the University of Cincinnati as a freshman in the fall. I'll obviously never run National Pipe, which had been our earlier plan. But that's OK, I'll be able to build a career elsewhere."

"And your brother?"

"He's taking some time off. Then he has to finish high

school and head off to college. I'm sure that's what will happen."

"Philip, anything you can tell us about these past several months? Ms. Knox's death. Your father's suicide. The banks basically taking over National Pipe."

"No. Not really. I'm trying to look forward, and not dwell on the past."

"Well, thank you, Philip. Good luck in college and our best wishes to you, your brother and your mother."

"Thank you."

"Well, 'ain't that sumpin', as they say on the prairie."

"What do you know about the prairie?" asked Ginny.

"OK. Not much. But that is good news about the company probably continuing to operate here."

"Sure is. Bet there're a lot of relieved employees."

"And their families."

"Also interesting, about the Van Hales."

"Yeah. The older boy seems to be doing OK. Who knows about his brother? And his mother. I've got my theory."

"Which is?"

"Ginny, I bet Van Hale left a separate suicide note for her."

"And?"

"And the note contained the account numbers and passwords for the various bank accounts where all the stolen money went. In Switzerland. Liechtenstein. Luxembourg. And who knows where else? She's probably making the rounds, picking up wads of cash as she goes."

"Could be. But I say more power to her. And to their kids. Heck, Joe, she must have gone through hell living with Van Hale, and then the embarrassment of all the dirty laundry coming out."

"Not to mention losing the company, including the future it would have provided her kids. Anyhow, since we all agreed to just let things be in regard to the murder and obstruction charges, and maybe even conspiracy, this financial stuff seems small potatoes by comparison."

"In fact," said Ginny, "other than the family losing the business, I'm not even sure who was hurt by the embezzlement, or whatever it was. He was really stealing from himself. The banks will get fully reimbursed when the business is sold, the one minority shareholder will undoubtedly get a good price for his shares, the employees and the city still benefit by the business operating here. Hard to envision a more victimless crime than this. Seems like only the perp and his family got hurt."

"Yes and no, Ginny. On the one hand, I agree with you that it's kinda victimless. But, we should also consider that the IRS and Ohio tax department are losing out with taxes never having been paid on those embezzled funds. So, we can call this victimless, or we can say these tax departments are the victims, and, in a way, that makes all Americans the victims. I know this is close to getting philosophical, but there is some truth to it. In any event, I agree with you. Let's let this one lie where it is. We'll leave it up to the IRS to decide whether and how hard to pursue this. I bet they'll seize as much as they need to pay any taxes due from Van Hale's insurance policies, as well as anything they get from selling the business and their house."

"I agree. And the Ohio tax folks, as they usually do, will

just take a backseat and tag along with whatever the IRS does or doesn't do."

"Fortunately, we have and will continue to have enough crime to keep us fully occupied. Imagine the boredom of being a cop where's there's no crime."

"Hard to imagine, Joe. But I don't think we have to worry about that. At least not in this lifetime."

"You have to wonder why a successful guy like Van Hale gets into all those extramarital affairs, embezzlement and who knows what else."

"Joe, I call it the 'celebrity syndrome.'"

"Which is?"

"It's a disease of all, or at least many, celebrities and very successful people: movie and TV stars; so-called sports heroes; big executives; and, of course, politicians. They wind up thinking that laws and social norms don't apply to them. They're above all that and can do whatever they want."

"I know what you mean. Remember that widow of a New York City super-wealthy real estate guy who said something like 'We don't pay taxes. That's only for the little people?'"

"Exactly. That's the perfect example of what I'm talking about."

"Gotcha."

CHAPTER 31

"**Y**ou almost ready?"

"Will be in a few minutes. Just need to brush my hair and put on my war paint."

"OK. I'm going to start the grill. I want to give it a lot of time to properly heat up."

"Joe, I gotta tell you. I'm scared to death."

"You hafta be kidding. All the scary stuff you've faced on the job for the past umpteen years, and you're scared of this?"

"Joe, except for occasionally having one or two couples over for dinner, I've never hosted a party like this. Plus, with all our co-workers coming, not to mention the chief and his wife, I really don't want to screw up."

"Don't worry, Ginny. You'll do fine. And I've got your back. Just like I do out on the streets."

"I know, but—"

"It'll be fine. Anyhow, I'll be doing all the barbecuing, so the overcooked and burned meat will be on me, not you. You bought the coleslaw and potato salad, as well as desserts. The salad you made looks fine. And drinks are easy. We're fully loaded with two kinds of beer and three types of wine. It'll be fine."

"I sure hope so. I do have to admit you had a good idea. A 'Spring Has Sprung' barbecue party for the department is a great way to socialize more with everyone. If nothing else, this should show the chief that we're really trying."

"Very true. It's great that all the detectives, except for Evan who's away this weekend, are coming. Plus, of course, the chief, Elaine from Dispatch and your secret lover, the desk sarge."

"And don't forget all the spouses or so-called significant others."

"I'm not forgetting. That's why I basically spent all my retirement savings on meat for today," said Joe with a smile.

About a month after Van Hale's suicide, Joe and Ginny had decided to host a barbecue for their co-workers. Joe came up with the barbecue idea and the 'Spring Has Sprung' theme. A month after the invitations were given out, party day had arrived. Given the relatively small size of Joe's house, they were fortunate with the weather. If everyone had to stay inside, they soon would have felt like caged chickens. The weather was still a bit cool, but with a lot of sun and virtually no wind, it was comfortable outside. Joe had borrowed a second grill and a bunch of lawn chairs from other detectives, so the place was as ready as it ever would be.

Guests started arriving a little after two, and everyone was there by 3:30. Drinks and snacks were enjoyed by all, and everyone seemed to be having a good time. Joe spent most of his time in front of the two barbecue grills, often assisted by other detectives. By four o'clock, everyone was well along with their eating, and compliments flew out to Joe for his burgers, franks and chicken, and to Ginny for everything.

At about five o'clock, no doubt encouraged by all the beer and wine that had been consumed, toasts and speeches began. Most dealt with thanking Joe and Ginny for the party, applauding the arrival of Spring and the day's current weather and, of course, the required teasing of each other.

To Ginny's surprise, a little before six, Joe stood up and said he had a few things to say.

"First of all, Ginny and I are delighted to have all of you here today. We all work together, but too infrequently take the time to socialize together. Plus, it's been great to get to know everyone's spouse — or whatever the current politically-correct term is for what used to be called boy-or-girlfriend. Secondly, I want to thank everyone who has accepted me into the department. I know now what a basket case I was when I first arrived. Thank you all for your patience and for, in most cases, putting up with all my shenanigans. And, Chief, a special thanks to you for not giving up on me. I know what a pain in the butt I must have been."

"Joe, why do you say that in the past tense? Things haven't changed all that much," said the chief with a wide smile.

After all the laughing and commenting died down, Joe continued, "Just one more thing and I'm done. Ginny, please come up here next to me. I have a question for you."

Ginny was a bit surprised, but she got up from her chair near the table holding the wine and wine glasses and walked over to Joe.

"Joe, if the question is whether you have to help clean up after the party's over, the answer is yes."

After everyone's chuckling died down, Joe responded, "That's what I assumed. No, that's not my question."

"OK, ask it already. These fine folks want to get back to partying."

"Yes, Ma'am. Ginny, you more than anyone has helped me heal. Without you, I don't think I'd be much different today than the mess I was when I first got here six years ago."

Ginny didn't say anything. But looking up into Joe's face, she gave him a sweet smile, while simultaneously feeling her cheeks turning red.

"Anyhow, to not drag this out any more, Virginia Harris, will you marry me? I love you and want you to be my wife." While speaking, Joe pulled out an engagement ring from his pocket and held it toward Ginny as he got down on one knee.

Ginny was shocked. Not about the love, but about the proposal. Ginny had assumed that, although she and Joe might eventually get married, Joe was not yet ready. In several ways, he was still living in the past, with that damn drunk driver killing his wife and son. She, however, had been and was more than ready.

Ginny was brought back to the moment by the loud cheers and clapping of everyone who was there.

With her cheeks redder than ever, Ginny responded, "Yes." She held out her left hand, and Joe put the ring on her ring finger, after which he stood up, bent down and gave Ginny a lengthy kiss.

With that the cheering and clapping started all over again, only louder than before.

Everyone had left by 7:30, and Ginny and Joe were done cleaning up by nine. Many things were washed and put away. Others were rinsed and stacked to await a thorough washing the next day.

Exhausted from the day, Joe and Ginny collapsed into bed around 9:30.

"Joe, needless to say, you shocked me today. How long were you planning this little surprise?"

"Oh, about five years or so."

"No, seriously."

"I don't know. It, or you, grew on me gradually."

"Jeez, you make me sound like a fungus. And when'd you find time to buy this beautiful ring? We're together almost constantly."

"I guess you hadn't noticed that my trips to the supermarket were taking a bit longer than they used to."

"You sneak."

"Ginny, we still have to figure out the wedding date, if it should be a big or private affair and all that stuff."

"Not to mention, finding a house, our house, to live in."

"Right you are. But I do know where I want us to honeymoon."

"Oh, really. Right to the good stuff. So, where should we honeymoon?"

"The Caribbean."

"The Caribbean? Why? I've never even heard you mention it before. You've never been there. And probably know as little about it as I do. So, why the Caribbean?"

"A couple of reasons."

"Namely?"

"Well, first, I froze my ass off this winter. As I get older, the winters up here seem to get colder and longer each year."

"And what if we get married in the summer?"

"There are plenty of other good reasons to visit an island or two down there. A lot to see and do. And eat and drink. Anyhow, I've heard that it doesn't get all that hot down there even in the summer 'cause of all the water moderating the temperature."

"OK. You won't have much trouble convincing me."

"And there's one more reason."

"Oh?"

"Picture us at some secluded hotel, with even a more secluded room. And with a hot tub or small private pool. Just the two of us — skinny dipping or whatever."

"You keep surprising me, Joe. You have a real romantic streak in you."

"Oh, yeah? Come on over to my side of the bed and I'll show you how romantic I can be, Mrs. McFarland-to-be."

Ginny smiled as she scooted across the bed.

Born in Brooklyn, NY, Stuart has lived in 7 states and 4 European countries. He and his wife now live in the foothills of the Blue Ridge Mountains. Stuart earned an engineering degree from Swarthmore College and an MBA from Harvard University. His career has included work for large multinational firms, small startups and management consulting firms. Stuart and his wife are instrument-rated private pilots and Stuart is a volunteer firefighter & EMT and a Red Cross Disaster Responder.

See what Stuart Safft is up to at his blog: https://stuartsafft.wordpress.com.

Other Books from Stuart Safft